A Letter From Thomas

A Letter From Thomas

Julien A. Fonte

MILL CITY PRESS

Mill City Press
2301 Lucien Way #415
Maitland, FL 32751
407.339.4217
www.millcitypress.net

MILL CITY PRESS

© 2019 by Julien A. Fonte

All rights reserved solely by the author. The author guarantees all contents are original and do not infringe upon the legal rights of any other person or work. No part of this book may be reproduced in any form without the permission of the author. The views expressed in this book are not necessarily those of the publisher.

Unless otherwise indicated, Scripture quotations taken from the King James Version (KJV) – *public domain*.

Printed in the United States of America.

ISBN-13: 978-1-54566-676-0

LCCN: 2019919893

Prologue

It started off as just another ordinary day for Mary Conti. Cindy, the middle-aged bank teller, repeated her question twice to the well-dressed yet frail Italian lady. As usual, she showed up every first Wednesday of the month to withdraw her Social Security check. And, as was her custom, she wore the same old pillbox hat with the bright pink cane that matched her purse. She prided herself in the fact that, at age 90, she still drove herself to the bank and back. Achieving accomplishments was her way in life and old age would not slow her down.

"Mrs. Conti, how do you want your money?"

Mary leaned forward and blushed at the embarrassment of old age. She wanted no one to know that she was hard of hearing.

"I beg your pardon." She spoke in a soft deliberate tone that mirrored an English accent.

Cindy repeated the question again. "Mrs. Conti, how do you want your money?"

Mary giggled at the confusion. "Oh. I see. I'll take twenties and tens. That will do for the time being." Cindy handed her the money. Happy and content, Mary put her money away and proceeded to walk towards the exit door.

"That is one bright cane." Mary looked up to a tall, elderly man who was hunched over his walker, both hands trembling from Parkinson's. He had thick, white hair and deep blue ocean-colored eyes. He was accompanied by a heavyset Hispanic aide with the name tag that read Milagros. He spoke with an English accent.

Mary smiled softly. "Thank you. It's easy to find. I've always been a fan of bright colors."

The old man glanced at her up and down, as if in deep thought.

Hesitantly, he spoke, with an almost bewildered expression as if denying to himself the thoughts he was formulating in his mind.

"I'm sorry," he said, coughing as if stalling for time to wrap his head around his thought, "I'm sorry... but could you ... ah..."

Puzzled, Mary asked, "I don't believe we have met before. Have we? Are you a teacher? I've taught all over Long Island." Mary wasn't sure if this man was genuine or a quack.

The elderly man gestured toward the leather chairs. "Have a seat please. You look awfully familiar. Please forgive me ...Is your name perhaps...Mary?"

Now Mary was suspicious. "Excuse me?"

"My name is Thomas Donahue. We were ..."

Mary dropped her cane. Her purse spilled all over the floor. James, the security guard, ran to her assistance. Milagros and James both got her belongings together and seated her across from Thomas. Mary looked like she had seen a ghost.

After reassuring James that she was a CNA and that Mary was fine, that she was just in a state of shock, James let her be. Milagros couldn't help but wonder what the story was between them. We're they ex-lovers? High school or college sweethearts? Something seemed curious to say the least.

Milagros turned to the old man. "How do you know her?"

The old man quivered and spoke solemnly, "Mary. You were my first love ... You were my friend ..." Mary cut him off.

"Thomas you're just a bunch of old letters," Mary blurted out without realizing the can of worms she opened.

The old man expressed genuine amazement, "Mary, all these years, you've kept them?"

Thomas was intoxicated with happiness.

"THE LETTERS?" Mary asked, as if denying their existence for but a moment, then replying with a slight but apprehensive pause.

"Yes, yes I did."

Milagros eyes widened in curiosity. "Letters? What letters?"

Neither one of them spoke. There was a brief but awkward silence.

Mary was flustered. "Never mind. I must be on my way." She started to slowly walk away. "It was nice seeing you Thomas."

"Love letters?" Milagros innocently inquired.

Thomas swallowed hard. "Yes."

Mary was despondent. She was in a state of shock. Her mind could not comprehend whom she was seeing. Was it really him? How was this humanly possible?

"This sounds interesting. You guys should get together and talk about it." Milagros was persistent.

Thomas raised his hand for her to be quiet. "Yes, we should. Mary, I'm 94. My health isn't good. I've got one foot in the grave. Let's go to the coffee shop next door. We can sit and talk and reminisce. Like old times."

Mary, overwhelmed by the moment, shot a quick, "No. I would rather not. It's best I get going."

The old woman mumbled under her breathe, "I can't believe this."

Thomas was taken aback. "No. You wouldn't?" He frowned.

Mary gave a forceful smile. "Thomas, you and I are strangers. We don't have anything to discuss. It was nice seeing you. A rather pleasant surprise, I'll admit. But I'm not interested in going back down memory lane."

Thomas gave her a puppy dog look.

"Mary, think it over. I don't mean to inconvenience you. I tell you what, I'll have Milagros buy us coffee from Starbucks and we could bring it over your house and just talk. Forget about the letters. If it's too much for you to bear, I understand. It's just that I haven't seen you in so long. At 94, I may never see you again." He tried to play the guilt trip.

Milagros enthusiastically joined in. "I would be happy to spend time with you guys. I love history, and this sounds so interesting!"

Mary gave it some thought. She was interested in catching up with Thomas, although she was not a social butterfly. "Not today. I'm quite busy. I tell you what, give me your number and we will talk. Most likely we can meet up sometime next week."

"Mary, I'm quite old now and sick. I don't have forever."

Mary took out a piece of paper from her purse and wrote her number down.

"You can call me and we will set up a date." Your aide is welcome to come."

Thomas gave her a look of disappointment. He had waited for over 60 years to see what became of his first true love. He could not bear the thought of waiting anymore.

Milagros wrote down his number and gave it to Mary, who put the piece of paper in her purse.

"Thank you. I don't mean to be rude, it's just that I have a lot to do today."

Milagros shook her hand. "I'm looking forward to getting to know you." Her hazel-colored eyes lit up.

Mary's expression gave off the impression that she wasn't looking forward to the visit.

"We shall see." Mary said under her breath.

Milagros backed off. She wondered why this woman was so standoffish. What had happened between the two of them? Her mind was bombarded with questions.

"I'll be calling you soon," Thomas said with a soft smile. He had often wondered what became of Mary.

Mary and Thomas got up slowly and walked toward the door. Both never thought they would see each other. Never. Never in their wildest dreams.

7:45 p.m.

Mary had fibbed. Her only errand was to go to the bank and then home. Sitting in her kitchen, she admitted to herself that she had wondered what became of the man from Indiana. The road not traveled would be revisited and talked about.

It made Mary feel uncomfortable indeed. Questions that had secretly been dormant in Mary's agile mind were suddenly brought back to life. Did he move on in life? Did he marry someone who was more attractive, more intelligent? She would have never imagined that in her old age they would meet up again. Did he want to continue the relationship? At 90 and 94, how many years would such a relationship last?

Such an absurd thought, Mary said to herself while watching Wheel of Fortune. As usual, she guessed the correct answer to each puzzle. That's what 37 years of teaching English will do to a person. Chester, her cat, had jumped off her lap. She headed to the kitchen for a cup of coffee when the wall phone rang. Probably a telemarketer. She let it go and continued pouring her coffee.

It rang.

And rang.

And rang.

Finally, after the fourth ring and slightly agitated, she answered.

"Who is calling at such an hour?"

The voice that had haunted the back of her mind for decades replied,

"Mary. It's Tom. I would love to come over and see you. Tomorrow if possible."

Mary shook her head. "Tom, you and I are strangers. We lived our own individual lives. There is nothing to talk about."

His voice quietly said, "We weren't strangers in the past. If I am such a stranger... then why did you keep the letters all these years? I just think we should talk and reminisce."

Mary cut him off. "There is nothing to reminisce about."

"Mary ... the letters let me see them please. I've wanted to see you in forever. God made this possible. Please just please," he begged.

"Thomas," Mary struggled to get her thoughts out. "I'm really not interested in us meeting up tomorrow or any other day. I tried to be cordial, but the past is the past."

There was a pause at the end of the line.

"Don't you think that it's uncanny to say the least that we met today?" Thomas was trying to persuade her.

After a slight pause, Mary replied, "Yes. It's unbelievable to think that we would ever see each other again. I'm glad we did. Now good night."

"God made this possible. I just know this to be true."

"You never really believed in God when we younger." Mary was surprised at his change of thought.

"Life has changed me. I know God gave us the opportunity to meet."

"I do find this very peculiar," Mary agreed.

Thomas pleaded with her. "Mary, please just one night. I understand we will never have what was or could have been …"

Mary cut him off. "Just one day. I admit I have often thought about you. But I don't want this to be a recurring visit."

"You have been a permanent resident in the back of my mind for the last 70 years. We don't have the luxury to plan for one day to meet up. Not at our age. We could both be gone tomorrow." His voice teared up.

Mary couldn't dispute that. She had never envisioned her being 90 years of age. Much less ever seeing Thomas again. It still did not seem possible that she and Thomas would ever meet up. Perhaps in Heaven but most certainly not on Earth. Life is funny, she thought to herself.

She gave it some thought. A visit with Tom sounded nice. Those letters he wrote were sentimental to her. You don't keep something hidden from your husband and son for almost 70 years if it had no value. Alright. Fair is fair, she thought.

"You guys can come over tomorrow around noon. You have my address?"

"Yes, Milagros wrote it down. Thank you." A much-relieved Thomas replied.

Mary smiled to herself. She had questions. She didn't want to come off as too eager.

"Thomas? I just have to ask." She cleared her throat.

"Yes, Mary?" His voice was shaking.

"May I ask, how did you recognize me? It's been nearly 70 years since we've last seen each other. I just find it peculiar that you knew who I was. All these years have passed, and you still recognized me. I'm impressed."

There was a slight pause and then a cough. "Your face, although wrinkled with time, has not lost its beauty. Your large and inquisitive brown eyes are the same as I last saw them."

Mary smiled. She had wished she could say the same for him. Old age had done a number on him.

"I just want to make one thing clear. We aren't old lovers trying to rekindle a lost love. We are old acquaintances who just happen to have met up at a very unusual location," Mary said as cordially as she could. She wasn't the smoothest at communicating.

He was silent on the phone. Then he spoke some chilling words that sent shivers down her spine. "We are acquaintances." He paused. "With a past. See you tomorrow." He hung up the receiver.

Mary hung up the phone then sat down in the swivel chair near the stove. Was it possible for strangers to become friends again? Or, was friendship like a flower which only bloomed once and then it's over? No second chances. No going back to what could have been.

One

May 6, 2010

"Be careful going up those steps," Mary warned with caution. It had taken a good ten minutes for Milagros to transfer Thomas out of her Honda Civic. All the while, Mary couldn't help but be sad to see him in this condition. The once tall, athletic, handsome man was now very feeble and frail. Each step he took was balanced out with a deep breath. He stopped to catch his breath, then slowly climbed up the three steps to her front door.

Once inside, Thomas was ushered into the living room where he sat comfortably in the antique bergère chair that complimented Mary's love of old-world charm. On the wall were various old black and white photos of family, all beloved, most of them deceased. On her fireplace mantle were two photographs. One read the year as 1949 and the other read 1983. Both photos read John Adams Elementary school grade 5. The first photo showed Mary as a younger woman in her prime of teaching. The latter showed a more tired 63-year-old woman.

The air inside was stale and musty which gave Milagros the impression that she didn't get out often or have much company.

"Do you mind if I open the window? It's such a beautiful spring day. Some fresh air wouldn't hurt," Milagros volunteered, walking toward the window sill.

Mary couldn't remember the last time she opened the casement windows that showed a view of her front yard.

"You'll just have to wiggle the knob. This house is old and decrepit like Thomas and I." She laughed at her own joke.

Nodding his head in approval, he said, "Nice place you have. Very cozy home. I love your collection of antique furniture and I adore your book collection. Really brings out the charm. You always had good taste."

Mary had gone to the kitchen and secretly blushed.

"Thank you. How do you two take your coffee?" Automatically Milagros replied, "Mr. Donahue likes his with cream no sugar. I like mine black."

"Very well. If you don't mind my asking. Why do you refer to him as Mr. Donahue and not Dr. Donahue? It's a sign of respect you know, young lady. While outside this door, there is very little respect in this world, inside my house there is respect. Especially for those that have earned it. He is a Doctor. In my house, you are to refer to him as Dr. Donahue. Do I make myself clear?"

Milagros nodded sympathetically of the old woman's request.

Thomas replied in a humble tone. "I haven't been in practice since 1992. She is my aide. Not my patient. Milagros has been my companion aide since my diagnosis of Parkinson's last November."

"You live alone?" Mary inquired, while reaching in the fridge for the cream.

Thomas responded with a sigh. "My niece and her husband own a house with an in-law apartment. About five years ago, I had a bad fall and broke my hip. They figured it was best that I move from Indiana to be with them. I never see them though. Doesn't make sense to me. You live in the same house, I'm the oldest relative they have. Yet they both work 80 hours in the city and only spend a half hour checking up on me. What about you? Do you have any kids?"

Mary slowly brought out a tray of coffee served in her fine china and three fresh croissants which she bought from the local bakery. Baked goods were her weakness. She just so happened to order an additional two croissants that morning. In her mind, it justified as a midnight snack.

"I have one son. His name is Paul. He and his family live in Connecticut. A lovely little coastal town by the water called Branford. About an hour and 20 minutes or so away."

"Do you ever see them?" Asked Milagros chewing on her croissant.

Mary was hoping to avoid that question, so she looked the other way, but she responded. "Very rarely. They have their own lives. I have a younger sister that lives over in the next town. Her name is Gina. She checks up on me quite a bit."

There was an uncomfortable feeling in the air. Almost a hint of sadness.

Milagros smiled. "That's good. At least you have some family in the area."

Mary shrugged her disappointment off. "I'm able to manage my independence. That's one thing I hope to never lose."

"I'm losing mine. It isn't easy. Especially when you're a man. I've lived a full 90 years, but only existed the last four." Thomas said in a quiet tone.

"What do you mean? You've only existed these last four years?" Milagros asked slightly puzzled.

Thomas looked at Milagros in the eye. "When you can't do anything for yourself. That's not living, that's existing. I'm sure Mary can attest."

Mary nodded. "I'm still able to fend for myself, though I have days where it's not easy. Yesterday was one of those days. I almost didn't make it to the bank."

"Thank God you did!" Thomas exclaimed.

Mary smiled. She still could not believe that Thomas Donahue was seated in her living room. She had naturally assumed that he was deceased all these years.

Thomas noticed the color Polaroid photo dated June 1985. It showed Mary and her husband enjoying a wedding. Her husband toasted towards the camera while she sat and smiled.

"What was your husband's name?" Thomas asked with no feeling of being nosy.

"Albert. He passed away in 1988. We were married for 39 wonderful years. He lost the fight to pancreatic cancer. That photo was at our son's wedding. My husband died less than three years later."

Not one to show emotion, Mary coughed to distract the tear coming down her face. "And you? How long has your wife been gone for? Or is she still living?"

Thomas quietly spoke, "I never married. After we broke up, I never found another one like you. There were women that proudly would have wanted my last name as theirs, but you were my world. My friend. My confidant. We had so much that could have been."

Mary retorted, "Stop it. You were a smart, handsome, young man. You could have had your pick of women. You just chose to be a bachelor. That was your choice."

Mary shook her head. How could such a talented wonderful soul not find someone to marry? It made no sense to her. Why should he blame her? Mary thought to herself.

"Broke up? How serious of a relationship was this?" Milagros piped up. Her face was full of wonder.

Mary sighed. Thomas said nothing.

"What happened?" Milagros asked trying to fish out the truth.

"Mary and I were engaged…" he paused and let out a sigh, "and things fell apart." Thomas was uncomfortable. Mary rolled her eyes.

"I really wish we don't talk about it," Mary said anxiously.

"Why do you think I came to see you?" Thomas asked somewhat perturbed.

Mary remained silent.

Milagros jumped in the conversation. "What broke off the engagement? I mean if she was the one. What ended the possibility of you two getting married?"

Mary was getting uncomfortable. "You guys are getting really personal. I invited you over to have coffee and look at the letters. Not rehash what could have or couldn't have been. We are both old washed up people. The days of love are long gone. I'm an old woman and you are an old sick man. It wouldn't do either of us any good to revisit the past. The past is the past."

"I wanna know why. It's a harmless question." Milagros looked at Mary, then at Thomas. Neither of them would give in. They were both acting like a married couple who would not speak to each other.

After a moment of unbearable silence, Thomas broke out.

"It was our parents. My family was well to do, eloquent and educated. And Mary's parents were..."

Mary cut him off. "I was the daughter of two Italian immigrants from the old world. My mother spoke very little English and my dad was a construction worker. We were very poor. I used to wear old clothes and I never fit in as a child with the other children. That was why I was determined to get an education. For me, it meant a new life. I never felt like I was an immigrant. Back then, the blacks, the Italian's, the Jews, were all lumped together and frowned upon. I knew I was an intelligent person and not just a throw rug. We were given no opportunity to succeed."

Thomas softly spoke, "Now Mary, that isn't true. Look at these two pictures. Of your first and last class of 5th graders. You pursued your dream. You defied the expectations."

Milagros and Thomas looked at each other. He had given her sound reason.

Mary shook her head. "I always felt like the black sheep of the family. Don't get me wrong, I loved my dad and he loved me. My mother resented the fact that her daughter did not want to stay home and cook pasta. My sister Gina did that and never worked a day in her life. Her husband was a stocker at the local grocery store. My mother thought the world of them. Who do you think took care of mother when she was eighty-eight and sick? I did. I drove all the way down to New Haven to help her out in her last days. She never thanked me. She never said I'm proud of you for going to college and making a life for yourself. She made me feel like an outcast for wanting a better life for myself."

She stopped to take a sip of coffee.

"It was so frustrating. My dad was one of the hardest workers I knew and yet he was cheated in pay because he was an Italian man with a strong accent. The other men got paid 1.75 an hour for their work. Wilkerson, the foreman, paid him and the other Italian man .75 cents an hour. They didn't even work half as fast as he did. Do you think I wanted that for my life? To be cheated out of my worth?"

"That doesn't sound right. Didn't the equal pay act of 1938 protect immigrants from unfair pay?" Milagros inquired.

Both Tom and Mary were surprised at her knowledge. Secretly, Mary didn't expect much from her. To her surprise, she was wrong.

"Young lady, my Father was in his 50's, desperate for work, and had a family to support. People took advantage of immigrants left and right. It wasn't until later that things changed for the better."

"Much later on." Thomas added shaking his head.

Thomas continued his thought, "Back then, things were earned not given away for free. If you wanted a bag full of groceries, you worked for it. If you wanted an apartment, you worked to pay for the rent. A whole different world than today." He shook his head in disgust.

Milagros nodded. She was enjoying this conversation. In her own life, she knew people that took advantage of the system.

"When the Food Stamp Act of 1965 was created it was designed to help the poor while they were looking for jobs. It was never meant for those and their offspring to live on it." Milagros added.

"You're quite the historian." Thomas quipped.

Milagros smiled.

Mary took a piece of her croissant and chewed slowly. "I find it so aggravating when I turn on the television and see all these immigrants complaining about this and about that.

Compared to how I grew up, these people have it made." She was on the beginning of a rant.

"How we grew up, you mean." Thomas corrected.

Mary nodded her head. She remembered all too well how bad things were if you were an immigrant. There was no respect. No equality. You felt less human than your peers.

Milagros sat up in her chair.

"That's not true. My family came from Mexico in the 1980's, and they had quite an issue adjusting to America. I don't think any immigrant had it easy coming to America. I do think that the anti-Semitism, the racial hatred, and the bigotry is mostly gone. Although there are more opportunities available, it will never be an easy transition. We did not get free food and a free place to live. My father worked hard to keep a roof over our heads and food in our stomach. I respectfully disagree with both of you."

Mary concurred. "You have a point. So you're Mexican?"

She crossed her legs and sat upright in her chair. This evening may not be so bad after all. She thought to herself.

"My father is full blood Mexican and my mother is Native American. They live in Arizona. They retired and moved about two years ago. They say it's much cheaper to live there."

"Who can afford to live in New York?" Thomas smiled.

"Did you come here legally?" Mary asked with no shame.

There was an awkward tension in the room. For a brief minute, no one spoke.

"Mary. That's very rude." Thomas sat up in his chair. He had expected more from her. "It's unbecoming of you to ask that."

"It's just a question. She doesn't have to answer." Mary defended herself.

"I don't think it's appropriate." Thomas mumbled.

Milagros was okay with it. She gestured for him to calm down.

"It's okay, I'm used to it. I'm asked that question a lot. Yes. Yes, we did. That was one of the reasons why it was so hard. We couldn't stay in Mexico. We had no choice but to leave."

"I'm glad your family abided by the law." Mary smiled in approval.

"Mrs. Conti. My family are good Christians." Milagros replied.

"Religion has nothing to do with it. It's a sense of morality." Thomas spoke up.

"I'm just saying." Milagros was not liking how this was turning out. "My family follows the law no matter how hard it maybe. It would have been much easier to come here illegally."

"It's easier said than done." Mary softly added. "I would much rather not talk about it." Her disposition changed from letter of the law to understanding the sad reality for many immigrants.

"You understand?" Milagros asked, trying to find common ground with this elderly woman.

"Pop often spoke about how hard it was to make a dime. I was just two when we came to America, so, I don't have any real recollection of coming over from Italy. I just recall how hard it was being different."

"Tell me about it." Milagros muttered to herself.

Mary glanced at Milagros. They had both found common ground.

Milagros changed the subject. "So, if they," Milagros paused choosing her words carefully, "Approved ...would you guys be celebrating your 60th anniversary this year?"

"No."

"Yes." They both answered opposite responses but in unison.

"No. For me to say yes, would mean that I regretted the marriage to Al. He was a good person. We were meant for each other. Thomas and I were college sweethearts that didn't work out. And that's okay. That's life. You move on. I don't regret the hatred we endured. I don't regret the marriage to Al. Or having Paul. Plus having two wonderful grandsons. I don't regret any off that. Now please, get on your way. I knew this was a bad idea." Mary picked up the dishes and brought them to the kitchen then opened the front door, gesturing for them to leave.

"I think it's best you two leave," She said, her eyes were aglow with deep emotional pain.

Milagros kindly refused, "Thomas needs a chance to say why he said yes. You need to be fair."

"I don't have to allow such nonsense in my house!"

"We heard you out. Didn't we?" Milagros reasoned.

Mary was fuming, "Oh, alright. I'll let him reply."

Thomas took off his glasses and laid them on the coffee table next to the *New York Post*.

"Because we were a good match. Mary had problems, as do us all, but her problems, I could deal with. I was the Band-Aid to her wound metaphorically speaking. It's okay to have problems. It means your human, I really do in my heart believe that I could have …"

Mary exploded. "GET OUT OF MY HOUSE!!"

She opened the door for them to leave. "I knew this meetup was a mistake. Please leave my house. I really don't need this drama!"

Thomas was defiant. "I'm not going anywhere. You saw how long it took me to come inside, plus I never saw the letters. Now sit down, chill out, and be civil. You never could communicate well."

"Excuse me! I communicate just fine. You guys just don't know when to stop." Mary yelled back.

Milagros stood up and unfolded his walker. "Perhaps we should get going."

Thomas stomped his foot on the ground. "No. I haven't seen those letters in 60 years. This is probably going to be the last time we see each other. This is most definitely the only time I'll get to see the letters."

Mary softened her disposition. "Alright. You'll have to give me a minute. No more questions. Do we have an agreement?"

Thomas nodded his head.

Milagros raised her hand like a timid 5th grader. "I have a question. Where is the ladies' room?"

Mary rolled her eyes. "Go around the corner. Fourth door on the right. Make sure you flush. The knob is a little lose." She excused herself and went down to the basement to retrieve the dusty box of long-forgotten letters.

"Well, here they are." Mary placed the dusty tin box on the coffee table. The letters spilled out on the table, although yellowed from age, they were still legible. Milagros carefully looked at the dates on the letters which were slightly smudged.

"1944. Wow that's nearly 70 years ago. This is amazing!"

"Be very careful, young lady. These are very fragile. The last time I took these out WW2 was just a few years over."

"I'm astonished that you've kept them all these years. This is truly amazing!" Tom had the same expression that a child has upon entering Disney World for the first time.

The elderly woman smiled, "These were of sentimental value. There was so much emotion, so much truth, that I just couldn't get rid of them."

"What about this one?" Milagros took out a blue envelope that lay behind the yellow letters.

Mary snatched it from her hand. "Never mind this one. It has no relevance to tonight. She stood up and placed the blue envelope on top of the book case.

"What does it say?" Milagros was curious.

"I told you it has no relevance to our discussion." Mary said in an annoyed tone. "We will discuss these letters only. Forget about that one."

Milagros and Thomas looked at each other, then shrugged it off.

Milagros pulled out her cell phone. "Mrs. Conti. I really enjoy this discussion. Do you guys mind if I record you guy's conversation about the letters? People need to know. This is something out of a best-selling novel. Two people in love. Writing letters to each other. It's kind of romantic."

Mary gave it an honest thought. "No. I don't want my personal life broadcasted. You're an aide. A very good one. You aren't a writer."

"Do you understand what a gem this is? It's not just two young people writing letters to each other over summer break. This was during one of the most historic times in America. People will absolutely love this story of how you guys met again after almost 70 years. Who knows it may inspire people to look in their own genealogy and find true stories that are worthy of being read?"

Mary was indignant.

"No thank you. Tom and I are no celebrities. We are just everyday people. I admire your zeal. I will admit that this would make a nice read. But, I would rather we don't go down that road."

Milagros was persistent.

"Mrs. Conti, I really do believe that this would make a bestseller. I could write the novel and you could help edit it? Or even a movie? Seriously, this sounds like the plot of a Nickolas Sparks novel."

"YOUNG LADY!! I SAID NO!!" Mary screamed. Her son and daughter in law had not known of her prior engagement to Thomas. That was a secret she had planned to take to the grave. It was the unknown reaction of her family that scared her the most.

"I have a name you know. I would prefer if you call me by my name." Milagros shot back. "I'm not exactly a stranger anymore. We have been introduced."

Mary stood up and grabbed a pillow for her back, then sat down.

"This is my house. If I choose to call you young lady, I will. You asked a question and I replied. When you ask a question, the answer may not always be what you are looking to hear. Do I make myself clear?"

Milagros rolled her eyes and sighed. She was genuinely disappointed.

The old woman's face softened. "I don't mean to be cross. I would just rather we keep this between ourselves. I don't want the whole world knowing of our relationship. I appreciate your enthusiasm."

Thomas agreed. "I admit this story would make a great movie. I don't want us recorded though. You are going to learn a lot about life tonight. You're going to learn about true love and the fact that true love doesn't always win in the end."

Mary gave a short awkward cough. "There are 132 letters combined. We will both be long gone by the time we review them all. I thought we could go over the ones with the most intrigue," Mary added, trying to divert the subject.

"Every one of them reads like a novel. Remember, that's how people communicated back then. There is a ton of emotion in these letters." Thomas noted. "Most of them were written well into the early morning on many a sleepless night."

"If it's really true love then shouldn't it prevail?" Milagros asked in wonder. She was stuck on that concept. "I mean you hear all the time how true love always wins in the end. Right?" There was an awkward pause in the conversation.

"Young lady. You are getting personal." Mary snapped. "I suggest you leave the matter alone."

Tom looked at Mary, then at Milagros. "Sometimes life and all its uncertainties are stronger than love itself. Not to say we didn't try. We gave it our all. It just wasn't enough."

"So your parents were the ones that broke it off?" Milagros asked Tom.

"Oh no. My family was happy to have her as a potential daughter-in-law. It was Mary's parents, her whole family really that gave us a hard time." Tom stiffened his upper lip. "We never clicked."

"Things could have worked themselves out." Mary quietly said.

"Now Mary, you know your mother would have given us nothing but trouble. With our hectic schedules and your family's constant disapproval, we would have ended up in an early divorce. Just no way." Thomas wiped a tear from his eyes.

Mary sat still. She remembered all too well. She remembered the fights. She remembered being emotionally torn between her love for Tom and her love for her family. It wasn't something she wanted to go back to. It was a painful memory that she never wished to be resurrected. Unfortunately, it was brought back. She had to deal with a regret that she had lived with for so many years. She learned to love her husband, Al, although at first it wasn't easy. She was a thinker, he was a talker. With Tom, there was a true connection.

Milagros was about to speak when her phone went off.

"Hello?" She answered. "Mr. Donahue. Your niece wants to know when you are coming home."

Thomas smiled in pure delight. "Tell her tonight is going to be a late one. I'm enjoying myself." Milagros corresponded the message to his niece.

"Now. Who wants to go first?" Thomas asked enjoying the moment. "You, or should I?"

Mary jumped on the opportunity. "I'll go. My story is better."

Milagros sat upright in her chair in ardent anticipation of what was to come.

Thomas laughed and sat back in his chair. He knew this would be a night to remember.

TWO

(MARY'S STORY)

The matronly woman looked at her eldest daughter in disgust. Her daughter was lost in a good read on the sofa. A beautiful young woman with chestnut brown hair, innocent brown eyes and an infectious smile. Surely, Mary Mascia would make the perfect Italian bride. If only she learned how to cook. Then she would have a handsome son-in-law to provide for her daughter. Philomena Mascia shook her head at her daughter and said in a heavy Italian accent, "Why you read? You cook. You 23 years old. Too old to be single. I don't like."

Mary rolled her eyes. "Oh Mother. I just want to be educated. Books make you smarter. You can get lost in a book and pretend you are somewhere else. Like instead of being in this junkie old house in New Haven. I can be faraway on a ..." Before she finished her mother slapped her across the face.

"You father worka hard so you no have ta wash a you feet and a you clothes in the river like a me. Your father saw good America. But it was a no easy. So don a change a who you are.

You cook a, you clean. You no go to this a books." She threw her hands up in the air and cursed in Italian and slammed her hand down on the table.

Mary shook her head at her mom. Why would anyone want to stay home cook and clean? Education was her future. Little did her mom know her acceptance letter to Columbia was hidden under her pocketbook in the hallway closet. She had wanted to wait until her father came home from work around 10:30 p.m. It was a stormy Thursday June night in 1943. The two-family house creaked and leaked. Mary, her sister and her two parents lived on the second floor. A young couple lived on the first floor. The young man worked for the railroad and had befriended alcohol. Tonight was a quiet night which is what Mary wanted. She knew her world would change for the better soon enough.

The sound of her father's heavy boots echoed up the stairs. The door to the living room opened and in came a smiling presence.

Sam Mascia was 55 years old and had the strength of a young man of 25. All day long he worked and toiled in the blazing hot unforgiving sun. Standing at 5'3" and weighing in at 135 lbs., most people overlooked him as a weakling.

"Papa. I have some good news!"

Sam smiled in delight. "Oh yeah. What is?"

Mary showed her father the acceptance letter to Columbia. Sam was overjoyed. "My beautiful daughter got a college! That a good! When you go?"

"The letters say school starts on September 1, 1943."

"Mary you gotta brains. Use a them. Teach a kids. That a good job, bestakind! Now go to bed."

Philomena stepped out of the bedroom. Her hair hanging down to her shoulders. "She need to cook. Not read so many books!"

Sam his usual kind self replied, "Philomena, please. Go a back ta bed. She teach a kids. That a good job."

Philomena grunted and slammed the door.

Sam turned to his daughter. "Now listen. We need to celebrate." He reached in his pocket and pulled out a crumbled dollar. "Take. It yours. Buy you a treat." He took the dollar and put it in his daughter's hand.

Mary looked at the dollar then back to her father. She could buy a lot with that dollar, but her family needed it more. "Pop, I can't ... you keep it."

Sam looked like a child who had dropped his ice cream and was scolded by his parents. "I work hard. So, you enjoy life. Take, please."

"Was this from Wilkerson? Or from another contractor?"

Sam sighed. "Yes, it was a from him."

Mary looked her dad straight in the eyes. Harry Wilkerson is a crook. Do you realize all the money you are being jipped from? If you weren't Italian, you would make 1.75 an hour. You work 80 hours a week. That's ... hold on." Mary did the math on a blank piece of paper with a pen. "That's 140 bucks you would make every two weeks." Instead, you and Luigi are only being paid 75. cents an hour which amounts to 60 dollars every two weeks. That's half of what you would normally make. That's criminal."

Sam knew she was right but did not want to jeopardize his employment. In the back of his mind he remembered how hard it was trying to find a job as a newly off the boat immigrant. He remembered the laughter, the ridicule that he faced in the early days. True his job was not great money but it was something.

"I know. I know. You don a understand how hard it is to find a work. They gotta the sign, no Italian, colored, or Jew. You eat don a you? You got a roof." As if in unison, the water from the roof started leaking and splattered on Sam's head. "The landlord say one a day he fix a the roof. What a he do with money I give a him?" Sam laughed and put the dollar down on the table. Suddenly the door swung wide open.

Gina had come home after a night of partying. This irresponsible woman was the one my Mother loved more, Mary thought to herself.

Gina had alcohol on her breathe, tossing her hair aside her face, she greedily grabbed the dollar. "Oh you're giving money out now! Thanks Pop!"

Mary snatched the dollar back and gave it to her dad.

"That's not your money! Pop worked hard for his dollar. Something you wouldn't know of!"

"I won't have to work. I'm gonna marry myself a nice rich Italian man. Who the heck wants to work anyway?" You heard what Mom said, us Italian women belong in the kitchen.

Making pasta, popping out kids. Not writing letters to Eleanor Roosevelt or Mahatma Ghandi like you did last year. Why would you give her a dollar? And not me. I'm the deserving one." She asked, hoping he will give in and give it to her.

Sam's face lit up with pride. "Your sister go to a Columbia, education. She gonna teach. I very proud."

"Mom's not." Gina knew it hurt her sister that she was her favorite of the two. She liked to rub it in.

"It donna matter." Sam replied. "I'm a proud. Now go. And let Marie celebrate her Columbia."

Gina not getting the point. "Yeah, but shouldn't it be your mother and I are so proud of you?" Gina grinned sheepishly.

"Gina!" Sam yelled. "It late, go to bed."

"Sure Pop…" She rolled her eyes and went to her room.

Sam turned to Mary and gently patted her on the back.

"Your Sister is a loose in the head. She a wish she had a you brains." Sam gently opened Mary's hand and placed a dime in her palm. He whispered, "Buy a you self an ice cream a soda after you a work?"

Mary couldn't resist the ice cream soda made fresh. For ten cents, you got three generous scoops of ice cream served in a large glass filled with cola.

Mary was not gonna miss Gina, her mother, or seeing her father get cheated out of his hard-earned money. She certainly wasn't gonna miss her job as a waitress. All those obstacles would soon be in the past…

But, she would surely miss her father.

THREE

Anna Kaplan always felt a sense of responsibility towards Mary. She and her husband, John, lived three blocks from the Mascia family. Anna taught at the local high school as an English teacher. Throughout the years, she had seen students come and go. None of them were as memorable as Mary. Mary Mascia was a very shy young woman. She was kind of clumsy, socially awkward. She never really fit in with the other girls. Mary was also one of her best students. A straight A student, Mary took her work seriously and diligently. And it showed. She was an exceptional writer. Anna enjoyed having Mary as a student. So, when the news came that Mary got accepted to College, Anna knew she had to buy her a special gift.

Anna lived in the large Victorian with the wrap around porch and white picket fence.

On this Friday afternoon, Anna sat on her rocking chair reading a book while enjoying the summer breeze. Out of the corner of her eye she spotted Mary walking the family dog Buster, a small adorable Maltese pup. She smiled to herself as

Mary clumsily tried to walk the stubborn dog who had wanted to take a seat.

"Mary. Come over here." Anna called her over. Mary waved and gave a nervous smile. Buster barked and happily came over to Anna, pulling Mary over seemingly against her will.

Anna smiled. "I heard you've got accepted to Columbia. How exciting! I always knew you would end up in an Ivy League university. You are such a smart driven young woman with a bright future ahead of you."

Mary blushed at the compliment. "Thank you. I'm looking forward to following in your footsteps. You've inspired me throughout the years. I hope to do the same to my future students."

Anna bent down to pet Buster. "You will. You are an amazing young woman with a whole lot to offer. I wanted to take you to Albrights. I wanted to get you a new dress to wear, for when you go to a party and meet the love of your life."

Mary laughed. "I don't … I'm not interested in Italian men." She got it out expecting a reaction.

Anna laughed at the ridiculousness of her statement.

"Honey, you don't have to marry your own kind. You marry someone who loves you for the beautiful soul that you are. The world is full of good men. Of all different races. Ethnicity doesn't matter. Unfortunately, to some it does. What matters is how he treats you, how he provides for you."

"I know. It's just my mother is so geared on me marrying a fellow Italian. I just don't know. She says if I don't marry soon, I'll end up as an old maid." She sighed heavily.

Anna laughed at the nonsense. "Young lady, you're only 23 years old. You have plenty of time to find your true love. Don't fret over petty little things. It will do you no good in life."

Mary looked down at the wooden deck in shame.

"You don't understand," said Mary.

Mary shook her head in sadness.

"I most certainly do understand. As a Jewish person, I have seen my share of cultural prejudice in my life. I have chosen to rise above it. So can you." She smiled gently.

"It's not the same." Mary mumbled beneath her breathe.

Anna was no stranger to pain. Just five years earlier an entire ocean liner named the St. Louis with 937 passengers, most of them Jewish were sent back to Europe on suspicion of them being spies. They had reached Miami and under FDR's direction, was sent back to the Holocaust where some 250 perished. That was a heated debate that lay in the back of her mind. She understood Mary's issue but she was not gonna let her act like only her people were victims of injustice. The event that transpired some five years prior struck a nerve with the Jewish community.

Anna's voice got firm. "Jewish mothers can be just as instigating as Italian mothers. My own mother wanted me to marry a well to do Jewish man. My heart fell for John, who at the time was poor and had little appreciation for his Jewish heritage. I don't think he ever stepped foot in a synagogue. That doesn't matter. We are both happily married. We have a good life. I don't have any regrets."

"You don't?" Mary sincerely asked.

Anna caressed her hair. "Sweetheart, you marry who you want to marry. This is 1943. Things have changed. Your Mother is from the 19th century in her thinking. You know I would never turn you away from your parents but on that note they are wrong. I want you to be happy when you find the right guy. Not feel guilty. Now take this little guy home and come with me. We are going to make you look beautiful."

Mary smiled. Anna always knew the right words to say. In a way, Anna was more than a friend, she was more like an aunt. Mary believed that Anna truly cared for her. More so than her own family.

A large older woman with the big curly hair and heavy makeup smiled as the two women walked through the door. Business had been slow and they seemed like two candidates for a dress. Judging by their appearance she doubt they could afford much. The two women were plainly dressed.

"Welcome to Albrights. How can I help you two lovely ladies? What's the special occasion? A wedding?"

"She's off to college…" Anna announced proudly.

The old woman was surprised. "Off to college? Wow! Good for you!" What are you majoring in?"

"I'm getting my master's in education. I'm going to be an English teacher."

"Wonderful. Let me show you what we got." The lady brought them to the back of the shop.

Anna intervened. "Actually. I saw the perfect dress, I was in here the other week. The satin yellow sleeveless slip-on gown. I think she would look absolutely stunning in it."

"Yes that is a pretty dress. I have some more in the back. Just follow me."

"I don't want to see any other dresses. The yellow dress would look absolutely marvelous on her."

"That cost $75. It's very expensive. I'm sure I'll find one in the back of the shop. I have some much more reasonably priced dresses." She had a condescending attitude about her that neither one could stand.

"Has it been spoken for?" Anna asked slightly annoyed.

The old woman laughed. "She could never aff…" She stopped herself just in time.

Anna gave her the 'you don't know me look.'

"It's a gift for her being accepted to Columbia. She's not paying for it I am." Anna rolled her eyes in sheer annoyance.

Mary's face was full of disappointment. This was typical of people in Connecticut. "Anna it's okay I don't need something so expensive."

"No. You are going to have that dress."

"Very well. The dress is up front. Give me a minute to take it off the window display. It's $75 dollars. The satin is straight from India. Gorgeous dress. It's just costly. And I'm not sure if it will fit you."

"I have money." Anna snapped back. "You aren't too keen on keeping your customers. Are you?"

Anna was a woman of modest means. She dressed simple and therefore appeared poor . She wasn't though with her husband working as an accountant and her job as a teacher they got by just fine.

"No. I'm just making sure. That's all. There's a fitting room in the back. Why don't you follow me?"

After trying the dress on. Mary could not believe the person staring back at her.

"You look absolutely stunning in that dress!" Anna exclaimed.

Mary giggled. "I feel so beautiful!"

"You'll have all of the guys wanting to court you!" The older lady said, genuinely happy for her.

Mary blushed. "I doubt that."

"Don't sell yourself short young lady."

Mary looked and felt beautiful in her new dress.

Anna and the older lady were in awe at the transformation. Mary knew this was just the beginning of a new life to come. Things were looking up. For once. For once she could smile and feel good about herself.

FOUR

Emily Alexander waited in the downstairs lobby for her new roommate. Her aunt had placed a call last month asking if she would mind housing her young friend while she went to school. Emily didn't mind. She had a two-bedroom apartment that was just big enough for her and another person. At 36 marriage wasn't an option. Her life was her job. Tonight, was her turn to work a 12-hour shift at the Bellevue Hospital in Manhattan. Any minute Mary was to arrive.

"Mrs. Alexander. She's here," Frederick, the doorman announced. Emily put down the newspaper and went outside to meet her new guest.

The attractive blonde greeted Mary at the door to her apartment building. The doorman carried her suitcases to the third floor for her. Mary thanked him. The man looked at her for a second too long then left.

"It's customary to tip the doorman. Don't worry though, he knew you were a student and poor." Emily smirked.

"Sorry. I'm not used to a doorman assisting me," an embarrassed Mary replied.

Emily waved it off. "Don't worry about it. You're just a small city girl in the big ocean now. I've heard some nice things about where you're from. New Haven sounds like a nice city."

"It is. It's rich with history."

"So is the hospital I work at. It's the oldest in New York. I wouldn't be surprised if George Washington showed up asking to check his temperature for a fever."

Mary chuckled.

Emily's apartment number was B6. It was located at the end of the narrow hallway. A middle- aged, well-dressed couple walked pass them.

"Good evening Mr. and Mrs. Johannsson. Off to the theater tonight?" Emily asked.

The couple nodded. "We're off to see the new Bogart picture, Sahara. It looks like a good one," the man answered while holding his wife's arm.

"I should hope it lives up to his last picture. Casablanca was well done!" The wife exclaimed.

"Bogart doesn't seem to disappoint his audience!" Emily responded, happy to see them take a break and enjoy their night.

The couple smiled and walked on.

Turning the key to the brown mahogany door, it opened to reveal a small living room with a little kitchen and a bathroom off the bedroom. There was a second bedroom with the door open showing a twin bed.

"It's nothing special. It's good enough for me. My aunt said you needed a place to stay. I don't mind the company though I'm rarely here. You'll have the place all to yourself."

Mary enjoyed the simplicity of Emily's apartment much like her family's back home. This made the transition easier for her.

"Go ahead, freshen up if you want. I'll be leaving soon. My aunt told me all about you. She said you're the quiet type, kind of a loner. You'll have your privacy here. I'm a nurse at Bellevue in Manhattan. Like I said before you won't see much of me."

"You aren't married?" Mary inquired innocently.

"Me married? Honey, I work long hours with decent pay. If I was married, I wouldn't have any time for intimacy. As it is, we do more work than the doctors." Emily rolled her eyes.

Mary nodded.

"I don't need a man in my life. I pay my own bills. Do what I want, when I want. I'm all set-in life." Emily had a roughness about her that made Mary wonder what happened in her past.

Emily pointed to the key on the top of the ice box. "This is your key to my place; you can come and go as you please. All I ask is that you refrain from smoking."

"I appreciate your hospitality. Really I do. I'm not a smoker so no need to worry about it. I'm gonna wash up and retire for the night."

"Go right ahead. I'll see you in the afternoon." She put on her coat and left.

FIVE

While the world was in turmoil, Mary's world was at peace. She wasn't oblivious to the world's distress. Two years prior she wrote a handwritten letter to Mahatma Gandhi asking if worldwide peace was truly attainable. Several months later she received a handwritten response from Ghandi himself. He wrote back with the thought that peace can only be attainable if we eliminate greed and wrongful desires.

Everything felt so foreign. In college Mary finally felt like she had found her place in life. For the past couple of years, she had fought the negativity of her mother's resentment. It had taken its toll on her, in more ways than one. She was now with people who were driven to succeed in life. She now had a purpose a goal in life that was attainable.

Her family mailed her 20 dollars a month. $10 went to Emily and Mary kept the other $10 for her personal needs. Mary didn't like the idea of her family giving her a monthly check but living in New York, there was no way she could afford to live on the money she saved from her part-time waitress job.

Everything cost more in the city. Back home, a dollar would get you two gallons of milk, a dozen eggs, a candy bar and a soda pop. Mary went to the crowded grocery mart near the apartment building where a dozen eggs cost 75 cents, one gallon of milk cost 82 cents. Whereas a Hershey bar cost 25 cents back home 25 cents would buy you a large milkshake with a side of fries at the local diner.

As she waited in line to pay, a disgruntled mentally challenged man wearing a ragged coat and a scruffy beard voiced his opinion to the uninterested cashier. "I say we bomb them all. Roosevelt is doing nothing for us. Absolutely nothing. Some country America is."

The lunatic kept muttering to himself as he left.

The unshaven heavy-set guy working the register shook his head and mumbled, "What a nut." Then he turned to Mary. He rang up her order and then said, "That will be 3.75."

"3.75? That seems so expensive." She only had four basic items.

"3.75!" The man repeated in a gruff manor.

"That can't be right," Mary mumbled to herself.

The man replied in an annoyed sarcastic tone. "Look lady, we're in a war! Everything goes up in price. Plus, this is New York. I don't know where you come from. But, here that will be 3.75."

Mary decided not to bother explaining she wasn't from the area. She paid her bill and left.

As she opened the door to leave, a familiar voice called out to her.

"Mary!" Mary turned to see Laura Crosby, a fellow classmate of hers. Laura's father, Nathaniel Crosby, was a successful attorney and owned a 10-thousand-square-foot mansion nestled in an affluent area of Long Island. Laura made sure people knew she was from wealth, an attribute that annoyed Mary.

"Laura, nice to see you!" Mary said, hoping to avoid further conversation.

Laura put her hand on Mary's shoulder and gave her an invitation.

"I wanted to invite you to the formal dinner I'm having at my folks house tomorrow night. I know it's a little short notice. The truth is, you're hard to get. I'm not sure if you can make it. If you can, that would be great. Some cute successful guys will be there."

Laura spoke rather quickly, and she gave Mary a warm smile.

"Oh no, I'm busy. Thanks for the invite though," Mary stammered through her excuse.

"Oh yeah? Doing what?" Laura inquired, knowing full well she was bluffing.

"You got me there." Mary felt foolish for being caught. Her shyness crippled her.

Mary wasn't one to socialize. She hated the concept of going to a large party. Though she wanted friends, friendships didn't come easy for her. It would make a nice reason to wear her dress.

"Hope to see you there." Laura waved and continued to walk down the block. She disappeared in the crowd.

It was 7 p.m. Mary was seated in a rocking chair, while Emily was making a pot of tea.

"I don't know why you're acting this way. Go and have a good time. Seriously, do they have fun where you're from?" Emily seriously questioned the girl's emotional health.

Emily sat crisscrossed on her couch, while Mary sat slumbering in the plush rocking chair.

"I want to go ... it's just I can't." Mary sighed.

"Why can't you?" Emily asked, giving Mary a cup of tea. She took out a bottle of honey and poured a teaspoon into her drink.

"I just get this intense fear around people."

"I am going to give you some tough love. If you never get out of your comfort zone, you'll never grow. You can do this. It's a formal. You go, you eat, you dance. You create a memory. Everyone knows about the Crosby mansion. It's gorgeous."

Emily pulled out the dress from the bedroom closet.

"You will look like Lauren Bacall tomorrow night in this dress!"

Mary smiled awkwardly. "Your aunt bought that for me in Connecticut. It really is such a beautiful dress."

Emily looked at Mary straight in the eyes. "My aunt is a woman of modest means. For her to purchase such an expensive dress, proves her love for you. It would be an insult if she found out that you never wore it."

Mary couldn't argue with Emily's reason. She had always wanted to be a social butterfly. She admired people who could strike up a conversation with anyone on the dime. Though she longed for friendship, she didn't want to talk about the topics that most young woman talked about. She wanted a friend who had a deeper sense of the world. She wanted to have detailed discussions.

"I'll go. I'll need you to drop me off though." Mary asked, feeling more confident. Emily was proving herself to be a good friend.

"What time is the party?" Emily asked.

"6 p.m. at the Crosby mansion. Please show your invitation to the doorman upon entering," Mary said as she read the invitation which required all going to dress their best.

"Be ready to leave around 4 p.m. It's quite a drive. I have a feeling, it will be worth it. I'll pick you up at 11 p.m. I have a wristwatch in my room if you don't have one. Just meet me in the front."

"Wouldn't that inconvenience you?" Mary asked, secretly hoping that the plan would fall through.

"Not at all. It's my weekend off."

"Oh great! That means you can come with me."

"No, I'm not gonna hold your hand like a child. You're a grown woman, you can go yourself."

Mary rolled her eyes at her sarcasm. "You're off? I don't see why you can't come. Perhaps you may meet someone. "

Emily burst out in laughter. "Not just anyone can show up at a Crosby event. The most elite are invited. Unless of course you're good friends with Laura." Emily gave her a wink.

"I barely know her." Mary muttered.

Emily gave Mary a warm smile.

"She must be looking out for you then. The property is stunning. It was built in the style of Versailles."

Mary replied in a humble tone. "Thank you. I really appreciate the pep talk we had. You take after your aunt. She is a very kind soul. As you are. It's getting late now, see you tomorrow."

"No problem, dear. That's what friends are for. I must get going. Good night now."

Mary excused herself and went down to lay on her bed. She couldn't sleep. The Crosby mansion was about 20 miles from Williamsburg, comfortably nestled on Long Island's north shore, also known as the Gold Coast and the playground of Manhattan's rich and powerful. Mary Mascia, a young daughter of two Italian immigrants would be a guest at such an exquisite event. That blew her restless mind.

SIX

Ebenezer Crosby built the Crosby mansion in 1815. It was originally built as a wedding present for his wife, Victoria. She had fallen in love with French architecture during their honeymoon in Paris. Yet, when offered to move, she declined, stating that New York was her true home. The mansion took eight years to make and cost about three million dollars to create. Marble from Tuscany was imported. Victoria had wanted a house modeled after the Palace of Versailles. It sat on eight acres of land and was a well-known landmark. In his will, Ebenezer required that no one who wasn't related to him was to live there. In the 127 years in existence, numerous Crosbys had resided there. Nathaniel Crosby, the most prominent attorney in New York, now resided there with his family.

Emily dropped off Mary in the front of the mansion.

There were fountains that greeted the guest. The house, the grounds, everything told of an old wealthy past. The entire property was full of happy people conversing with one another.

There was a well-dressed man with dark, slicked back hair wearing white gloves and a top hat.

"Welcome to the party. May I see your invitation?"

Mary was so overwhelmed by all the lights and sounds that her mind was in a fog. Never would she think that a poor immigrant from New Haven would be invited to such a spectacular event.

The man repeated himself again. "Miss, I need to see your invitation, or else I can't let you in. The public isn't welcome. Guests only."

Mary apologized repeatedly. The doorman told her not to worry about it and let her in. Other young well-dressed couples excused themselves and walked past Mary.

"I love your dress!" A young woman noted while holding her boyfriend's hand.

"Thank you. It was a gift." Mary smiled. She had never been given a genuine compliment before.

"Looks great! Enjoy your time!" The girl flashed her a smile and kept walking on, disappearing in the crowd.

"Miss, would you like some caviar?" The young waiter asked. "We also have the finest wine for our guests. May I suggest the Chateau Talbot? It's one of the most popular wines of the year.

"No, thank you. I don't drink." Mary shyly replied.

"Very well then. Enjoy your time."

Inside everything was beautifully arranged. A large crystal chandler hung from the ceiling and there were scores of young men and women enjoying each other's company. The men wore tuxedos, while the woman wore their finest dresses. Three men played the violin while one musician was playing an unfamiliar piece of classical music on the Steinway piano. The mansion looked more like a museum than a house. She almost felt bad for Laura. How could anyone live like this Mary wondered to herself quietly.

She walked past a morbidly obese man who resembled the late President Taft. He had two gold handled canes and wore a monocle. "As was the usual, my horse won the race. Another two hundred bucks in my wallet. Did I tell you about my recent trip to Africa? I had two lions killed and stuffed for my collection," the man boasted.

The young gentleman he was speaking with was exceptional in appearance. He was tall and lean, and his hair was reddish brown. There was something about him that was different. Out of the corner of her eye, she noticed him checking her out. There are many beautiful women here. Why would he think I was anything special? Mary thought to herself.

The young man nodded his head. "Yes, I remember. You almost lost your son to malaria on that trip. That was in '39?"

"Excellent memory. And the doctor said I was too old and out of shape to go hunting." The man took a sip of his wine and chuckled to himself.

"Mary! Good to see you. I'm glad you made it. You look beautiful!" said Laura as she gave Mary a hug and introduced her to her fiancé.

"This is my husband-to-be David. We met last year while I was on vacation in San Diego. He is an astrophysicist."

"Impressive. Where did you go to school?" ask Mary, who was genuinely impressed.

"Pleased to meet you. I graduated from Yale in '33. Laura has family out in the West Coast, and we met at a party and here we are today. We are going to be getting married in the fall." The young man extended his hand out to Mary.

Laura smiled and said, "I couldn't be any happier in life. Is your boyfriend here?"

Feeling put on the spot and speaking rather fast, Mary replied. "I'm not seeing anyone for the time being. It's been nice seeing you guys. I'm gonna step outside for a bit."

"You feel okay?" Laura inquired, genuinely concerned.

"I'm fine. Just a little hot. I'm not used to being in a large crowd. It's overwhelming to say the least."

"You sure? Can I get you some water? Would you like to take a seat? You do look a little faint," David asked with genuine concern.

"I'm fine. Thanks, guys." Mary smiled awkwardly.

"Well, if you need anything at all, just let one of the wait staff know. They will be happy to help you. It was nice seeing you." Laura waved goodbye, and David escorted her to talk with friends of his.

Maybe there is something wrong with me. 23 and all alone. Maybe my mother was right all along. No man would want me. I'm too serious. I'm too shy. I'm too smart. I can't relate to people. My mother used to say that to me all the time. I was all brains and no personality. What am I doing here then? Negative emotions began to cloud Mary's mind. The combination of the music, the laughter, the people who were normal socially was too much for Mary. Frustrated, she looked for the nearest exit. The place was jam packed with people. Smiling happy people. And she wasn't. Deep down there was a void, an emptiness that only a man could fill.

"And then there was the food in Rome. Such small portions," The obese man kept going on. 26- year-old med student Thomas Donahue had kept his eye on the mysterious young lady who walked past him not really saying much to anyone. Something was wrong. There was a certain attraction to her that he could not get out of his head. JP Longfellow was a successful banker and known to talk till the sunset, an expression they used back in his home state of Indiana.

"Mr. Longfellow, I have to get going. I'll talk to you later. Please excuse me." Thomas excused himself and went outside to look for the young woman in the bright yellow dress.

"Was it something I said?" Mr. Longfellow said to himself. He quickly grabbed a handful of pig in blankets from the waiter.

Sitting alone by the fountain, thinking all to herself. Feeling out of place and out of touch with everyone. Missing her Pop and knowing that she wouldn't see him for a while. Everything seemed to come crashing down at once on Mary. The cool summer breeze blew through her hair. Her thoughts were interrupted by an unfamiliar voice.

"Nice dress, hon," said an elderly woman walking past the fountain.

Not wanting to look up, she said in a depressed tone. "Thanks."

"Miss, are you okay?" The voice belonged to the gentlemen Mary had eyed not too long ago.

Mary just sat there in a daze. Secretly, she had hoped that the two of them would leave.

"Miss, is everything alright?" Thomas repeated a second, more concerned time.

"I just want to be let alone." Mary's voice shook.

"Are you sure you're okay?" asked the old woman standing in the distance.

"I'll take care of her," Thomas volunteered, suggesting with his eyes for the old woman to leave.

"I'll take my leave," the old crone whispered in his ear. "She doesn't look well, if you ask me."

Thomas shrugged his shoulders.

The old woman walked away.

Except for the young couple kissing near the fountain, all the other guests were in the mansion, enjoying the night.

"Miss, are you alright?" Thomas asked again, in a kind and gentle tone.

Mary willfully ignored him. She was lost in her own world.

"Seriously? Is everything okay?" Thomas asked, taking a seat next to her.

"You don't know me! Go away! Let me be!" Mary snapped.

"Actually, I do." Thomas grinned. "You're the princess they talk about in the fairy tales that's waiting for her prince charming. I also know that you're very intelligent. They don't accept dumb bunnies at Columbia. I know that you're a driven person."

"How did you know I attend Columbia?" Mary asked, unsure of who this character was. "I just find it peculiar.

"People talk. And let's just say some people we apparently both know talked when I asked them about you ... and uh ... I liked what I heard."

"You must be friends with Laura? I really don't know anyone around here."

"Who don't they know? I'm surprised Winston Churchill isn't here tonight." Thomas quipped.

Mary laughed. There was something about him that captivated her interest. "And what gives you the impression that I'm a princess?"

Thomas thought about it for a minute. "Well, for one thing. I've never seen a dress that beautiful before. Only someone of royalty would wear that."

He got a smile out of her. "Who are you? I must know who my knight in shining armor is." Mary asked playing with him.

"My name is Thomas Donahue. These rich fancy parties give me a headache. I came outside to get some fresh air, and you looked like you needed someone to talk to."

He gave her a sincere smile.

Mary glanced at the man who was seemingly concerned.

"What are you a psychiatrist?"

"Uh, no. I'm not. I'm a doctor though. Well almost. I'm just starting med school at Yale, but I don't think I'll finish up at Yale." Thomas looked down at the ground then up at Mary.

"How come?" inquired Mary.

Thomas shrugged. "I'm just a country guy. I don't really fit in with these New Englanders."

Mary twirled her hair. "I notice you have a slight accent. Are you from England? I always felt people with English accents seemed more intelligent."

Thomas laughed. "I hope I don't disappoint you."

Mary piped up. "Obviously, you're intelligent. There's no disappointment to be had. Were you born in England?"

"I was born in England. My family moved in November of 1919 when I was 3. I don't know much about England, except that the food isn't all good. I was raised in a small town in Indiana. My father is a successful surgeon. So, this kind of lifestyle I'm used to. Truthfully, I loathe it."

"Really?" Mary's eyes widened. He was a few years older than her. She could deal with that.

"Yeah, rich people have no experience in life. Everything is given to them. Plus, I find them kind of boring. My Dad would have me come with him to these clubs that are exclusively for the rich. I would go and sit and listen to these men talk about politics, stocks, etc. All the while they would puff on their Cuban cigars. It was terrible. The man you saw me talk to,

JP Longfellow repeats the same stories repeatedly. He really is a bore. A fat bore at that."

They both laughed. There was a chemistry between them like no other man she had known.

"Your statement about rich people having no experience in life seems like a contradiction. You mentioned your father is a successful surgeon?" Mary asked, trying to see what his reply would be.

"Who was the son of a factory worker. My father worked hard in life to get to where he is now. He wasn't given any kind of financial support for his schooling. He worked hard and made his dream come true."

Mary nodded her head. "I see. That makes sense now."

"Enough about me. I don't even know your name," Thomas smiled.

"Mary. My name is Mary Mascia. I'm from Connecticut. New Haven, it's a small city," she giggled to herself. "How foolish of me. You told me you went to Yale?"

Thomas seemed interested in every word she had to say. His eyes lit up. "I know nothing about New Haven or Connecticut for that matter. Except that the weather is lousy, and the people are difficult to please." He smiled. "Go on, tell me more."

"It's quite true. The weather is unpredictable, and the people aren't always so pleasant. What would you like to know? Ask away."

"I wanna know, what is your dream. What is your passion?"

Mary stopped to think for a second. "I love to read. I love to write poetry. I love to learn. That's why I've always wanted to be an English teacher. My dream would be to travel the world."

"I traveled to India last May. Interesting country it is. Fascinating people, great food. You know the anxiety you deal with. They have herbs that can cure it."

Thomas sat back and enjoyed their discussion. It was apparent that this girl had a good head on her shoulders. She seemed like she was the one. Sure, there were more attractive woman then her, she was unique in every sense of the word. She had an innocence that was different about her.

"Really?" Mary asked in wonder. Her social anxiety had always crippled her.

"Yeah, I've used it myself."

Mary was surprised. "You have anxiety? You seem so ... put together."

"I've been through stuff," said Thomas as he shrugged his shoulders.

"Who hasn't? Times are tough. I doubt it will get easier." Mary smiled.

Out of the blue, Thomas asked, "Is it true you wrote to Gandhi?"

Mary put her hand over her mouth trying to suppress her awkward smile.

"Who told you? I don't believe I shared that with anyone. Seriously, who told you?" Mary was suspicious.

Thomas grinned sheepishly. "Laura told me all about it."

Mary was puzzled. "I don't recall that ever being brought up in conversation."

"You did write to him?" Thomas inquired.

Mary was not one to openly communicate especially to a stranger. He seemed sincere though.

"Yes ... I did." Mary quietly replied.

"That is amazing! About what in particular?" His eyes were full of amazement.

This woman was his type. She had problems that were unseen to the naked eye. To the outsider, she was shy and withdrawn. If you dug below the surface, however, she was a young woman full of wonder and intelligence. The saying still waters run deep perfectly described her, Thomas thought to himself. Her problems were manageable. He could deal with her shyness.

"I wrote to Gandhi about the issue of world peace." Mary giggled nervously to herself, unsure of his reaction.

"That's amazing. I always wondered about that issue myself. Why can't humans just act normal and get along for goodness sake. Did he respond?"

"Yes, he did. Surprisingly six months after I wrote him, I received a handwritten reply. He explained that true peace was attainable if we all put aside our greedy nature and worked along with each other."

"Interesting. Seemingly impossible. I think the world is too corrupt to ever accomplish peace on its own." Thomas looked at his watch, then at Mary who had a dreamy look in her eyes.

"I imagine that one day the world will achieve peace. Nothing is impossible." Mary said trying to see where this would lead.

"I don't think we will ever see the end of this bloody war." Thomas shook his head.

"Time will tell." Mary said with a positive spirit.

"You know, I would love to get to know you." His eyes lit up.

Mary laughed. Secretly, she was intrigued by this man. He had kept her interest.

Thomas put his arm around hers.

"Why don't we go back inside? We can continue our discussion tomorrow. Have you ever gone horseback riding?"

Mary looked at Tom with a sense of uncertainty.

"I would like that. As far as riding a horse, I can't. I don't know how."

"Oh, you must come. There is this horse farm not far from here. A lady owns it, and for two dollars an hour, you can ride a horse throughout the most beautiful pasture."

"You'll have to teach me how to ride." Mary replied while watching his reaction.

"Sure! I ride all the time back home in Indiana."

Mary liked the idea. She was drawn to this man for reasons she was unsure of. Was it his appearance? Was it his kind demeanor? Was it his ability to draw me out of my shell? Was it a combination of all three? My family would never allow us to be married. If it should get that far. Why should they decide who I should marry? It seemed ridiculous but it was my reality.

My parents had a certain control over me. Like a puppeteer controls his puppet. Think this, Mary. Say that, Mary. Love this, Mary. Hate this, Mary. It seemingly never ended.

"I would love that." Mary's whole face lit up.

"I could pick you up tomorrow if you want or I could give you the directions."

"I live with a friend in Williamsburg. It's rather far."

"Do you have a ride home? I could take you home tonight."

"No. Don't be silly, my friend is going to pick me up at midnight. I wouldn't expect you to pick me up tomorrow. That's much too far of a drive."

Thomas smiled. "The nearest functional town is 45 minutes to an hour away from where I live back home. Trust me, I have no problem picking you up. Just give me the address and time and we will make it happen."

Mary was hesitant. "Don't you think this going too fast? We just met. I really don't know you. You don't know me. I'm sure there are plenty of other young women who are worth getting to know."

"True. How many of them have written to Mahatma Gandhi? Mary, you are unique. I see a future with you. You have captivated my mind." Thomas got lost in Mary's eyes.

"No. I can't. You don't know me well enough to even pursue a relationship. I know where this is going." Mary stammered.

"Actually, I know a lot about you. You're highly intelligent. You're funny. You have the most beautiful brown eyes in the world. That's all I know so far. I wanna know more. If you let me in."

In her mind she mused. He does seem like a nice man. It would be nice to get to know him. Mary sighed within herself.

"Fine. I don't want to rush into something I'll regret. I came up here to pursue my studies not to find a man." Mary nervously replied.

"We will pursue our studies together as friends." Thomas quickly replied.

Mary smiled uneasily. "I assume you have a good memory."

Thomas fumbled in his pocket and took out a pen and a business card. Mary wrote down the address and handed it back to him. He gently reached for her hand and took her inside.

Once inside, an elderly man who recognized Tom asked "Mr. Donahue. May I take you and your lovely woman's photo?"

Thomas laughed. "We just met. Sure." He put her arm around her waist. She and her whole spirit was illuminated in pure happiness. The picture would be a real keeper in the decades to come.

SEVEN

The horse farm was located on a rural area of Long Island. Young happy couples came from all over to ride on the picturesque pasture. Sadly, the war had taken much of the business away.

A middle-aged woman of small stature noticed the cherry red Pontiac Torpedo Six coming up the hill of her rustic farmhouse. Thomas had phoned the house earlier in the day reserving two of her mares. He offered to pay a handsome fare for the day.

As Thomas parked the car in front of the house, the thin woman with gray hair stood up from her rocking chair. She took a sip from her iced tea and proceeded to go down towards the young couple.

"You must be the lovely young woman I've heard all about."

The woman extended her hand out to Mary. "My name is Nora Lindley. My husband and I have run Lindley Farm for 25 years. I understand you guys are gonna do some riding today. Well, let me show you your horses. Follow me."

She took them around to the horse stalls. Mary had never seen a horse up close before. The majestic creatures intrigued her. They looked at her with wonder.

"I'll assign you to Honeysuckle. And your friend to Dixy." Thomas thanked her and gave her a wad of one-dollar bills.

"Honeysuckle is a tad stubborn but I'm sure you can handle her." Nora warned Thomas. He was a common site at her farm. Whenever he was in the area, he made sure to stop by. She wasn't worried about him. His girlfriend seemed utterly afraid of the horse. Poor thing Nora thought to herself.

"I'll be fine." Thomas smiled while petting the horse.

"And will you be alright?" Nora asked Mary.

"Well, actually I never...," Mary stammered.

Mary was about to reply when Thomas spoke for her.

"She's with me. I'll take care of her."

Nora chuckled. "I should have known better. You're in the company of Dr. Donahue. You guys enjoy your day now. I'll see you in a few hours. Just knock on my front door when you two are done."

Nora happily counted the money. It was enough to make ends meet. Times were tough, and most people simply could not afford to spend money on horseback lessons. As a devout Protestant, she viewed this as a gift from God himself.

Thomas helped Mary on her horse. Her mare was white with a black spotted eye. She chuckled at the thought of her on a horse. The open field ahead of her looked like freedom.

"You know how to make the horse stop? Just give it a pull on the reigns. Now, let's test these horses out." He gave the horse a good kick. "Yeah!"

Mary was timid about riding fast.

"Come on, give her a kick. Kick her hard. And say, yee ha!" Thomas coaxed her riding off screaming like a kid in a pool.

Mary gave her horse a strong kick and the horse took off. The feeling of the wind blowing through her hair, the reassurance that she found a guy who seemed to appreciate her for who she was, that combination delighted Mary.

The young couple rode for what felt like an eternity both equally enjoying each other's company. Upon entering the woods on the other side of the meadow, Thomas finally spoke.

"Mary slow her down. We're gonna go near a brook. The horses like to stop and drink up." Thomas had gone through this trail many times before. He befriended the Linley's oldest son Luke who had gone to war and came back in a coffin. That's why he was happy to give Nora a large amount of money. The Linley's were good solid people.

"Wow. This was such an amazing ride. Thank you. How did you know about this place? It's off the beaten path." Mary was really impressed with Thomas. They talked about everything under the sun that afternoon. Thomas made her laugh in ways that no other man could.

Thomas sat up on the horse and let it finish its last gulp of water. A frog hobbled on past the distracted horse, followed by a white hare.

"I was friends with their son, Luke. We met at a bachelor party for a friend of his. He was off to the war and never came back."

"That's so sad. How old was he?" Mary now understood why Nora seemed distant.

"Just 22. He was killed in battle. Shortly after his birthday, his body was shipped back home, and his ashes were cast to the sound." Thomas shed a tear thinking about Luke.

"These zealous young men go off to war and come home in a casket. If they do come home their minds are often left behind. As a medic, I have seen the worst of the worst. Stuff I wish never to speak about."

"War is so evil," Mary stated shaking her head. "And unnecessary."

"War is a part of life. Unfortunately," Thomas stated.

"It seems like you know everyone," Mary noted, genuinely surprised. She was trying to change the morbid subject.

"Not everyone. I don't know your family."

Mary laughed hard. "You would love my father. He's a kind soul like you. My mother and my sister, well, they're a different story. My mom wants me to be this Italian stay-at-home wife that does nothing but eat, make kids and cook for the family. That's not me."

"No, that's definitely not you. Even I know that. You're a learner, you're an iconoclast. Like in my life, my family wanted me to marry these privileged, snobbish, no personality type of women. Just because their daddies got money."

This man really does know me, Mary thought while cherishing the moment to herself.

"I wonder if your family would approve of me. I'm letting you know off the bat I'm not well off, nor is my family," Mary spoke nervously.

"Oh, don't worry about it. You are a kind, beautiful soul. I'm sure my family will grow to love you."

"I should certainly hope so." Mary was aglow with happiness.

"How about your folks? Imagine your folk's reaction when you tell them you met a doctor." Thomas grinned.

Mary looked the other way. "I would rather not think about it."

Thomas was confused. "Well, why not?"

Mary grimaced at the thought of her parents discovering her potential relationship with Thomas.

"Mary is there something wrong?" a concerned Thomas asked.

"You aren't their type. Let's not talk about it. This afternoon was such a delight." Mary tried to put on a fake smile. She could see the pain in his eyes.

"Not their type. They don't even know me." Thomas mumbled.

Mary annoyingly blurted out. "Wait a minute, Tom, we just met. We're already talking about meeting the family? Isn't it a little too soon?"

Thomas held a steady gaze straight ahead.

"Mary, in this crazy uncertain world, when you meet someone that you know is just right for you, it's never too soon. There's no time to waste."

"There is so much truth to the words you just spoke," Mary spoke softly. He had captivated her interest.

Thomas was silent and looked at Mary. They were riding back to the farmhouse, taking it slow. He was savoring every moment with her.

That day would end with a beautiful sunset and a first kiss. The relationship would blossom quickly.

On the surface, everything seemed so euphoric. The letters would lay claim to the progressive intellectual relationship that these two would develop between them, seeming to fulfill a need that lay deep inside. Thomas was fully engaged in his medical studies. Though he started at Yale, he would finish up at Kansas State University. Thomas was more at home with the Midwest. Mary was starting her career as a teacher looking forward to her educational journey.

Things were looking good for both of them.

However, in the back of their minds, an issue would ebb at their emotions, deep down the obvious issue could not be ignored. Her parents. A discussion that neither one of them looked forward to, needed to be had. Many weeks would go by before either one would tackle the issue. The letters filled with passion expressed for each other as well as for the tumultuous events that engulfed their world would come almost daily. The issue of her parents though could not be solved through the written word. They would later meet up and tackle the thorn in the flesh that caused both of them anguish.

Several Weeks Later

It was a beautiful Saturday afternoon in August. Thomas had come up to Connecticut for the weekend. Mary and he would enjoy an afternoon at the world-renowned Savin Rock Amusement Park. Mary had been eagerly awaiting to see her love.

The sound of children's laughter filled the air. People came from all over America to escape the reality of the war for a few hours of fun. It was so nice to see people of different cultures enjoy the pleasure of the amusement park, Mary thought to herself.

"Hot dogs! Get your hot dogs! 25 cents!" shouted a heavyset man pushing a cart. "Can I get you a hot dog, sir?" the man asked Thomas.

Not one to eat hot dogs, Thomas normally would have declined. The atmosphere, however, seemed perfect for a nice split dog.

"Thank you, I'll take one." He grabbed some lose change from his pocket.

"What about your lady friend? Would she like one? Best hot dogs in Connecticut. We cook them split. It makes all the difference," the man proudly stated.

"No, thank you. I'll take some cotton candy. How much?"

"Normally, that will be a dime. For you, I'll charge a nickel," the man grinned.

"Here, take a dime. I wouldn't give every pretty girl a break. You need to make some money pal." Thomas said giving him the dime.

The man smiled and handed Mary her cotton candy.

"It's very good," Thomas noted, wiping off the mustard from his face.

"You missed a spot. Right above your upper chin." She took a napkin and gently wiped his face.

"See how much I need you. I would have gone around looking like an idiot," Thomas said smiling.

Mary laughed, then she blushed three shades of pink. He was such a handsome man she thought to herself.

Mary was holding his hand. Everything seemed so ideal. School had been going well. Her anxiety about life had quieted down. She knew the inevitable had to be faced. Surely Thomas wouldn't bring up such a sensitive issue on such a relaxing day. Or, perhaps he would. He seemed nervous. That wasn't like him. She was the one with the problems. Thomas seemed to have all the right words. Perhaps he would bring up her parents, Mary thought to herself as she ate her cotton candy.

"This is such a pretty beach. I've never been down here," Mary chuckled.

"I thought you grew up in New Haven?" Thomas was genuinely surprised.

"I did. We were just too poor to ever enjoy an amusement park, so we mostly stayed home. This is so nice. It's such a beautiful day." The summer breeze blew through her hair.

"It doesn't cost anything to enjoy the beach," Thomas joked. He held her hand. Mary looked unusually beautiful today, he thought to himself.

"We were both too embarrassed to be seen with our old raggedy clothes. My Pop would give us both ten cents for an ice cream soda. That was our treat. We used to get it at the pharmacy a few blocks from our home."

Mary sensed something was wrong. Thomas had a distant look in his eyes. Something was troubling him.

"You seem awfully quiet. Are you okay?" Mary asked.

"I'm fine." Thomas spoke in a solemn tone.

Mary gently lay her hand gently on his. "I don't think you are."

Thomas had not looked forward to this moment. It needed to be said. The reality of her parent's disapproval had to be addressed. Why here? Why now? Thomas kept asking himself. Why ruin such a beautiful afternoon? There was no other time. His mind was tormented day and night over this moment.

Thomas cleared his throat. "About your father ..."

Thomas paused for a moment choosing his words.

"What about him?" Mary asked, hoping he wasn't going to bring up her folks.

"Do they know about me?"

"Yes, of course. They know I've met this wonderful man from Indiana. Mary really did not want to pursue this discussion.

"Do they know there is a cultural difference between us?"

Mary shook her head and looked away. "I don't want to talk about it. Not here."

Thomas knew this had to be addressed. "We need to talk about it. This has given me restless nights. I can't deal with it anymore. Do they know?"

"No, they don't." Mary stammered.

"Why not?" Thomas snapped.

"I just couldn't. You don't understand how hard it is for me. It's something I really can't explain." Tears started coming down her face.

Thomas sighed. "It's quite simple. I wish you wouldn't make such a ruckus out of it. All you have to do is say 'hi mom, hi pop, I met this wonderful man who's from Indiana who happens to be an Englishman.'" Thomas was unsympathetic towards her, in his mind, irrational dilemma.

"You really don't get it? Do you?" Mary was sincerely hurt.

Thomas gave her a comforting hug and a soft kiss on the forehead. "Everything will be okay."

"I doubt it." Mary wiped away her tears.

"You know I love my folks. My dad's a doctor, my mom is a homemaker. Life hasn't been easy for us. My folks separated for two years while I was in high school. Things are better. As much as I love my folks, I must do what's best for me. In the end, it's what's best for Thomas that matters. You need to adopt that mentality."

"Easier said than done," Mary replied, looking down as a seagull stood near her feet. She pushed it away.

"Don't say it, just do it. It's your life. Remember that." Thomas believed in her. He knew she could get through this.

"Thank you. I needed that reassurance." She awkwardly smiled to herself.

"You were saying that your parents split up? That's terrible." He had seemed so composed, as if life had forgotten to give him any problems. He is much stronger than I am, she thought to herself.

"It was the worst two years of my life. It's over and done with now. I still remember my Dad asking us kids who we wanted to live with, Thomas sighed.

"No child should have to decide which parent to live with," Mary agreed with a deep sigh.

"Eventually, they reconciled and got back together. It just took time." Thomas had his head down. The painful memories were coming back to mind.

"That's terrible. I mean, I'm glad everything worked out." Mary couldn't imagine not having her parents together.

"Just forget I told you. I was just making a point that every family goes through dark trials. Just as my family survived, so will yours. If life taught me anything, it's that the bad won't always stay bad, and the good won't always stay good."

Mary pondered those words. The bad won't always stay bad, and the good won't always stay good. Comforting to hear but unrealistic for their situation.

"That's a good saying to live by. I just hope this won't pass. I mean us. You and me. I hope our love for one another will never be replaced with the bad."

Thomas shook his head. His mind was lost in deep thought.

They were seated at a bench enjoying a pinkish sunset. Bing Crosby was playing on the background speakers. Young couples were happily dancing the night away. The sound of children enjoying the rides was in the air. It seemed as though everyone but them were happy.

After a few minutes of thinking silently, Thomas spoke,

"You're a grown woman. When you're a child, your parents decide what you eat and what you wear. They decide which form of schooling you receive. As a grown woman, they do not decide whom you should marry."

"Oh, you just don't understand." Mary replied. "It's complicated."

"No, you're just afraid." Thomas said shaking his head in complete confusion.

Mary knew he was correct. She also knew how controlling her family was. Her mother especially.

"True. What do you do when your family has such a strong influence on you? We could never be .... more than friends."

"Is that what you want?" Thomas asked while looking her in the eyes.

After a brief pause Mary replied, "No. I want this to work out. I want to pursue this relationship."

"We aren't engaged yet. Do you wish to go down this road? Or should we just let it be. I'll go back home, and you'll never see me again. Is that what you want?"

Mary kept silent.

Thomas took a sip of his Coca-Cola.

"Mary, I asked you a question." Thomas said slightly aggravated.

"Will you please just let it go!" Mary snapped.

"Yes or no?" Thomas asked.

Mary knew she wanted a life with Thomas. You don't meet someone of his caliber every day. Thomas was a rare, one of a kind man. She felt comfortable with him. Their minds were alike. He made her feel like a truly beautiful person. There were so many reasons why and one powerful reason why not. Her parents. Her mom.

"You aren't exactly what they want. They want a young strong Italian Catholic who works all day with a hammer and a nail in his hand."

Thomas replied quickly. "I'm young and I'm strong. Granted, I'm not Italian nor do I believe in Catholicism. As for work, the hammer and nail may not be my choice of profession but being a doctor will allow us a life of financial ease. Surely, that must be of importance to your folks."

Mary sat still. She was lost in her own thoughts.

Thomas gently rubbed her shoulder. "Don't you worry; we will get through this."

Mary shook her head as tears of frustration were coming down her face. Thomas handed her a napkin.

"It's what they want. I love my family. I've never been one to disobey." Mary said, fighting through the tears. "It's always been what they want."

"Is it what you want? That's what truly matters."

Mary sighed deeply. "No, it's not what I want. I just don't know."

Thomas gave her a hug.

"If they really want their son-in-law to be Catholic, he paused. I will gladly convert. If that's what it takes to win their approval and most importantly win you, Mary, my love. Then that's what I'll do."

"Don't be ridiculous. You don't change faiths to please another person." Mary smiled at the ridiculous thought.

"I think God would understand," Thomas replied, looking at the water, then back at Mary.

There was a moment of silence. Thomas was lost in his thoughts while Mary was trying to contemplate how this issue would work it's self out. There was no solution.

"Still ... it wouldn't work." Mary stammered through the tears.

"Why? If you love someone and they love you? Why should it matter what anyone thinks? I'm willing to change my faith just so I can earn your family's respect and that still isn't good enough?" Thomas felt comfortable enough to express his feelings.

"Tom stop. You don't know my family. You don't know my mother. Please, I'd rather not talk about this. Besides, you're from Indiana. You have a life out there. I have my life here." Mary was getting defensive.

She knew Tom was right. She also knew her mother would raise all hell if she brought home a man who wasn't Italian. Unfortunately, her fear of her mother was stronger than the power of reason.

"Alright, just leave me out of the equation. Suppose you met someone from New Haven. A non- Italian man who loved you for the wonderful person that you are. You guys courted. And he proposed. A great big beautiful diamond. Biggest diamond they make on the market. You would still not go through with it? Because your Mom wouldn't approve?"

"TOM STOP IT!" Mary started to cry hysterically.

"Are you okay?" asked a young mother with two children. She had been quietly observing the couple from afar.

"She's fine. We're just going through something," Thomas explained. His eyes reassured the woman that all is well.

"Things will get better. Keep your chin up." The young mother smiled and walked away.

Through tears, Mary smiled at the woman's sincerity. She meant well. But things would not get better, they would get worse, Mary thought to herself. Much worse.

"Tom, I love you. I really do. I just don't know what to do."

Mary sighed deeply. She wiped her tears from her eyes. She had never felt such a strong sense of frustration.

"I know what to do. I have the perfect solution. I meet them. They have no reason to like a person they never met. Once they meet me, everything will be fine. We will be on our honeymoon to the tropics." Thomas cracked a smile.

"It won't go well," Mary spoke, fixing her hair.

A seagull was near her right foot and again, she gently kicked it away.

"You don't know that. Your father will see that I'm a very swell kind of guy," Thomas assured her. He did not want Mary having the slightest doubt.

"When will I see you again?" Mary asked knowing he was leaving for Kansas in the morning.

"I can come back next month. I promise." Thomas took a sip of his Coca-Cola.

"Can or will? There is a difference." Mary corrected.

"I will be back." Thomas leaned forward to kiss her on the lips. Mary wouldn't have it.

"Next month? Thomas why couldn't you just stay at Yale? Letters just don't do any justice. Neither of us can afford to keep spending the money we do on telephone calls and letters," Mary pouted.

Thomas couldn't argue the truth. It was costly trying to mail letters every week from Kansas to Connecticut. The long-distance telephone calls were much too expensive. But things would eventually work out Thomas kept reminding himself.

"Honestly, I feel so out of place here. I'm more at ease in Kansas. It's a whole different atmosphere. One day you'll see for yourself. Why don't you just come out with me?"

"I wish I could," Mary said in all seriousness.

"Why don't you? Connecticut is a beautiful state, but the people aren't nearly as friendly as down where I'm from," Thomas stated.

"Everything and everyone I've ever known is up here. It would be hard to just get up and leave everything behind."

The two of them were walking by the water holding hands. It was a windy day and the tide was coming in. Mary always loved the sound of the waves crashing against the shore.

"Sometimes you just have to get out of your comfort zone. I never in a million years would have thought that a small-town country boy would be dating a beautiful and sophisticated Connecticut girl." He held her hand softly.

"Oh, stop! There's nothing remotely sophisticated about me." She blushed at the compliment.

"Mary, you are one of the most intriguing women that I know of. Perhaps intriguing is the wrong word. You're deeper than you appear. You have so much to give."

She laughed. This young man truly understood me. Mary thought to herself. He knew how to make her feel better. He completed her.

Mary looked at her watch. It read quarter past 5. Dinner was always at 6 p.m. "I think it's best we get going. My mother sets the table for 6 p.m."

Thomas led Mary to his car. He looked into her beautiful brown eyes. There was fear and a sense of sadness.

"Don't worry about this. Things will work themselves out. They have to," Thomas said with a touch of doubt.

He opened the passenger side door. Mary sat in the front and adjusted her hair.

"You don't seem so sure," Mary noted. They were about 10 minutes away from home. Thomas had borrowed his friend's car for the night.

"You can never be sure in life about anything, just hopeful. We can hope for the best." Thomas was quite for the rest of the drive to Mary's home.

"I don't want to be unsure. I want to be sure," said Mary quietly. They pulled up to her home when she saw her father on the porch, smoking a cigar. He just stood there. His eyes were staring into the distance, unaware that they had pulled up.

"Please don't say anything to Pops. Next month you'll have ample opportunity to get to know him. Just let me off," Mary spoke softly.

"Don't worry. I'll save the drama for next month." Thomas pulled right in front of their house. He locked eyes with her father who just stood there. Thomas bent over his seat and kissed Mary on the lips.

"Not here! I don't want him to see us being affectionate."

Thomas was taken aback. "I can't give my girl a goodbye kiss?"

"Not with my father standing right there. I'm tired and don't want any problems tonight."

Thomas shrugged his shoulders, "I understand."

"Write back to me when you get home. I love you." Mary said nervously, she could feel her father's disapproval.

"I sure will." He took off. Mary watched him turn the corner and drove away.

"Hi, Pops," Mary said as she gave her father a hug.

"Who's he?" Sam asked, in his characteristically gruff voice.

"My boyfriend."

Sam coughed up some phlegm. He spit on the ground.

Taken aback by Mary's words he proclaimed, "We gotta meet him. When you bring him here?"

"He's coming back next month. He wants to meet the family."

"Oh yeah."

Mary smiled awkwardly. "Yeah it will be nice. You'll like him."

Sam looked at her and spoke the words Mary never wanted to hear. "We meet, I don't know if we like, but we a meet."

"We've already arranged for him to come," Mary shrugged her shoulders.

"Have him come. We eat. We see," said Sam turning his back and abruptly heading upstairs to his room.

Mary followed him inside and nervously closed the door behind her. The weeks leading up to the visit would be full of restless nights for them both.

EIGHT

Next month

Anna Kaplan had just finished setting the table for her guests when the doorbell rang. A nervous looking man with a handsome build was standing next to Emily, Mary's roommate and Anna's niece. Mary was coming up behind them. Her posture was straighter, her whole demeanor had changed. She looked like the definition of confidence.

"Come on in. The food is still cooking in the oven." After embracing her niece, she then turned to Thomas. He was clearly nervous about meeting the future in laws.

"How do you do? My name is Anna Kaplan. And yours?"

"My name is Thomas. Thomas Donahue. Mary and I met a few weeks ago at a party. She suggested it would be nice if I met her friends and family," he said, giving her a warm smile.

The man looks like he walked off the set of a Hollywood movie. Seemed to be the ideal match for Mary. They both looked like the ideal couple, Anna thought to herself.

"Well, I'm glad to meet you. Please make yourself welcome. Have a seat and relax. Would you care for a drink?" Anna asked. "My husband keeps his own miniature bar in the cupboard." Anna smiled, hoping it would put him at ease.

"Sure. That sounds nice. I'll have a scotch." Thomas wasn't much of a drinker except for rare occasions. This was certainly a rare occasion. Finding true love was as rare as it got. He was nervous about meeting Mary's family. Mary and Emily had gone to the kitchen to help with the final dinner details. Her family was coming soon. He hoped that all would go well.

Anna poured some scotch out of the bottle, then handed Thomas the glass.

"My husband will be home in a few minutes. He's an accountant. Mary tells me you're a doctor. How exciting! What's your practice?"

"Not quite yet. I'm gonna be going into cardiology."

"Cardiology? I think that's fascinating. The heart is such an interesting organ." Anna took a seat across from Thomas. She placed her drink on her new read, "A Tree Grows in Brooklyn."

Thomas cleared his throat.

"It's amazing how much we have to learn," he added, seeing that the conversation was a little dry. He asked her how she knew Mary.

Anna lowered her voice. "We moved here in the fall of '31. Mary was 11, then a very smart young thing. I had her as a student in high school. I teach 10th grade English. She was one of the brightest students I've ever taught. What I really mean is that she's a very deep thinker. She needed someone like you in her life."

Anna already knew he was the one for her.

"Thank you. She is quite an exceptional young lady. Honestly though, I'm a little nervous about her family."

Thomas was cut off short by a knock at the door.

Anna opened the door to reveal a smiling Sam Mascia. His wife, dressed in all black, stepped in and smiled.

"Thank you. Where is this?"

Philomena stopped herself short and studied the young man in front of her. Not saying a word, her eyes shot daggers at Thomas. Samuel noticed and gently put his hand on her shoulder.

"Philomena pleasea."

Thomas offered up a friendly smile. "My name is Thomas Donahue. It's a pleasure to meet you. Your name is?"

Philomena stood still, lost in her own mind.

Sam shook Thomas hand. "My name is Samuel and thisa my wife, Philomena. You a good guy. You a Doctor?"

He spoke with an old, unsophisticated Italian accent.

Not allowing Thomas to reply, Philomena broke her silence. "I hatea doctors." She scowled like a mad dog.

"Scuseame." Taking his wife aside on the front porch, Sam looked his wife in the eyes. "Nostra figlia non ci ha mai dato motivo di preoccuparsi. Maria è una ragazza meravigliosa. Tu sai che quest'è la verita. Chi siamo noi per dire di no? Pensa

che con la sua educazione e il che lui e' un dottore, non possiamo sapere mai della destina che capitano."
(Our daughter has never given us any reason to worry. Mary is a wonderful girl. If he happens to be the one. Who are we to say no? Think about it, with her education and his being a doctor, they may never know of the struggle that we have had.)
Philomena scowled at her husband. "Non ho nemmeno sopportato la lotta in America solo per avere nostra figlia che buttava via la sua eredità. È già abbastanza brutto che voglia andare al college e diventare insegnante. Ora sposerà quest'uomo che non è nemmeno italiano? Dice che viene dai soldi. Le persone con denaro non ci rispetteranno. Non abbiamo nulla. Lo sposerà e poi dimenticherà tutto di noi. Gli uomini italiani sono fedeli alle loro mogli. Non mi piace per niente."
(I did not endure the struggle to America just to have our daughter throw away her heritage. It's bad enough that she want to go to college and become a teacher. Now she gonna marry this man who's not even Italian? She says he comes from money. People with money won't respect us. We have nothing. She will marry him and then forget all about us. Italian men are loyal to their wives. I don't like at all.)
Samuel looked his wife straight in the eye. "Devi smetterla!! Anna ha lavorato molto duramente per farci un buon pasto. Mary ha atteso con ansia questo giorno da un mese. Il minimo che puoi fare è essere calmo e rispettoso. Non ti farò dominare questa sera. Quindi siediti e mangia il tuo cibo. Personalmente Mary potrebbe portare a casa un uomo di colore e non me ne

importerebbe. Finché ha un lavoro e la ama. Perché dovrebbe importare che cultura è? Non lo conosci nemmeno."

(You need to stop!! Anna has worked very hard to make us a fine meal. Mary has been looking forward to this day for the past month. The least you could do is be quiet and respectful. I will not have you dominate this evening. So sit down and eat your food. Personally, Mary could bring home a colored man and I wouldn't care. As long as he's got a job and loves her. Why should it matter what culture he is? You don't even know him.)

Philomena grunted in disgust. "Prima di andare a questo Collegio, poi incontra questo medico! Sarò stasera tranquilla, ma questo non significa che io approvo!!!"

(First she go to this college, then she meets this doctor! I'll be quiet tonight but that doesn't mean that I approve!)

Samuel looked his wife straight in the eyes. "Non staro ' qui a litigare tutta la notte. Ti ricordi una cosa! Se non fosse stato per il mio lavoro come un cane, saremmo ancora vivere in quel vecchio villaggio sporco. Non hai fatto niente per farci arrivare qui. È nostra figlia. Se vedo che questo Donahue la tratta il modo in cui ti ho trattato tutti questi anni poi lei dannatamente bene può sposarlo."

(I'm not gonna stand here and argue all night. You remember one thing! If it wasn't for my working like a dog, we would still be living in that dirty old village. You've done nothing to get us here. She's our daughter. If I see that this Donahue treats her the way I treated you all these years, then she darn well can marry him.)

Out of the corner of Sam's eye, he saw John Kaplan's car pull into the driveway. John gave a friendly wave from the driver's seat.

Samuel pleading with his wife. "Pleasea, be quiet."

"Ah!" Philomena threw her hands in the air. She was livid. How dare he tell me how act? She thought to herself. Mentally, she feared one thing and that was change. She knew Mary wasn't traditional.

"Mr. Mascia. Is everything okay?" John Kaplan stepped out of his car. He looked at the angered expression on Philomena's face.

Samuel smiled at John and said. "Is good, is good."

"Your wife doesn't look very happy. Are you sure everything is going well?" John was genuinely concerned.

"Donta worry." The old man put his hand on John's shoulder. "Let's go and eata."

They went inside. Everything was far from good. In Sam's mind, this would kill his wife if they wed. Which is why it could not happen.

Anna's dining room table could seat 12 comfortably. The aroma of Italian cuisine was in the air. It was a smell that was foreign to Thomas. Back home in Indiana, Italian food was a foreign delicacy. To see the sauce be freshly poured over the homemade stuffed manicotti; the redolence of freshly baked Italian bread filled the room, Tom knew this was no longer just

A Letter From *Thomas*

rich men talking about a food so foreign to the meat and potatoes Tom grew up eating as a boy. If marriage could be possible, he would eat this wonderful food for life. Philomena had spent the good portion of the day cooking and showing Anna how to make certain dishes. In return, she tried to prepare her for what was to come. She said that Mary was a sensible person who wouldn't rush into something. Philomena wouldn't hear any of that.

Sipping his wine, Thomas said, "This food is excellent. Italian food is the best. I've been all over the world. Spain, Portugal, England, Africa, Italy, China, you name it. The best food is in Italy. Which part are you from Mr. Mascia?"

Sam cleared his throat, "We born in Cafizzi, small town, mountain town. Gotta married in nineteena fourteen. We coma here 1921. Beena here eva since."

"I can't say I've heard of Cafizzi. I'm sure it's a beautiful town." Thomas said trying to make Sam feel comfortable

Sam and his wife grunted.

Could this night get anymore awkward? Thomas thought to himself as he took a sip of wine.

John Kaplan wiped the sauce from his chin with a napkin and asked, "So tell us about yourself. You're from England? What's it like over there?"

Thomas replied quickly, "Frankly, I don't know much about England. Except that it's cold and rainy and the food tastes lousy. My family left for Indiana in 1919. My dad had an aunt that lived out there. So, that's where we ended up. I was only three at the time so I couldn't really tell you why we moved."

The table laughed. Philomena sat there eating her food slowly, shooting daggers with her eyes at Thomas once again. Anna sat next to Philomena and tried her best to be the diplomat between the two of them.

"Where in Indiana are you from? I don't think any of us have been past Delaware," She chuckled at her own joke.

Thomas was still chewing his food.

John jumped in. "I don't really know much about Indiana. Please tell us." He smiled at Thomas.

"I come from a small town called Noblesville. It's secluded. My family has an old farm house that goes back almost one hundred years. It's a great house, lots of character. I guess you could say I live in a cow town. I love it though, lots of great hardy people. Small town people with big dreams. It's mostly a farming town."

"I see. I grow a food myself. My backa yard is a full of fruitas and vegables. You want an apple, I'll give an apple. You want a pear, I give a pear." Sam cocked his head back. He was known for his impressive variety of produce. Neighbors would often insist on giving him money for his work. He would always say, "Take, eat. Ahh, it's the bestakind." A man of few words, his love was his garden. He often spoke of his vegetables like people. Referring them to Mr. Lettuce or my friend, the tomato.

"You should see the bottom of the barrel fruit they give us back home. They charge too much." Emily, who had been quiet that night, decided to chime in. She was rooting for Thomas in her own mind. He deserved her and she needed him.

Thomas laughed. The tension finally started to lessen.

Thomas was happy that he got off to a good start with his future father-in-law. Or so the illusion told him. The mother would have to give in.

Samuel cleared his throat. "Tell me. You a gooda Catholic?"

Thomas never expected that blunt question. "Well, I follow the Pope in the news. I was raised a Christian. My friend back home is a minister."

Samuel wasn't satisfied with the answer. "Let me tella you this. No a Catholic, no a marry my daughter."

"Pop!" Mary shouted across the table.

Samuel shrugged his shoulders. "Whata can I say? You a Cath-o-lic, no?"

Anna cleared her throat. "I think that nowadays it doesn't matter what you believe in. A good person doesn't have to be of a certain faith. If you truly love someone. That's all that matters."

Samuel shook his head. "Notta in my house. Donta like." He said in his gravelly voice.

"We aren't exactly getting married just yet," Thomas nervously replied.

Samuel laughed to himself and rolled his eyes. "Why you come here? If not looking to marry my daughter."

"Well, we're just friends. We just thought that it would be nice for everyone to meet each other." Thomas was nervous, uncomfortable. He unbuttoned his top collar.

Samuel threw his hands in the air.

"Love takes time." Anna added, hoping the tension would subside.

"Indeed, it does." Mary agreed.

"How old are you?" An unfamiliar voice that hadn't spoken much that evening finally asked something. It belonged to Philomena.

"26." Thomas answered, wishing things would loosen up.

Both parents were aghast in disgust.

"Mary is only 23. That's too old."

The entire room was silent. Anna looked at her husband. Emily was trying to think of ways to change the subject.

"Mom! Papa! Will you please stop it!"

"Is true!" said Samuel, taking a sip of his wine.

Anna came to Mary's defense. "If I may speak. Your daughter is not your typical 23-year-old woman. I should know. I see many immature young people taking things like marriage and courtship too fast without weighing out the costs. I think your daughter and Thomas are to be commended. She took the time to bring him over here to meet you guys. He seems like a perfectly intelligent, well-rounded young man. You may have your differences, but you must learn to accept people for who they are. Not for who you want them to be. It goes both ways.

There has to be a certain amount of respect. I see it in Mary and Thomas, but I don't see any coming from the two of you."

"She's our daughter. If we donta like, then there it goes," Philomena snapped back.

"Aren't you older than your wife?" Anna asked Samuel.

Samuel sighed. "I born in '87 and she born in '90. It donta matter."

"I think it's quite foolish for you two to make an issue out of something that you did yourself. I know English isn't your first language, but you do understand where I'm coming from? You see my reason?" Anna wasn't sure how well his comprehension was.

Samuel grunted. Philomena nodded forcefully.

"It not same." Philomena replied angrily.

Thomas bumped his knee on the table as he stood too quickly. "I don't like where this is going. I'm afraid I'm going to have to leave."

"Thomas! No!" Mary pleaded.

Thomas gestured for her to be quiet.

"I love the food and I love Anna and her husband's hospitality. I think it's quite lovely that they opened their home. I just can't sit here and be treated like I'm an unwanted hobo. Forgive me for becoming frustrated, that's exactly how I feel, darn it!"

"Sit down, Thomas," Anna said surveying the situation with her eyes.

"I can't!" Thomas replied with mixed emotions.

"Can't we all be civil?" Emily exclaimed. She had been taking it all in and praying to God to help her stay calm.

"It's no use trying to educate them. They can't help how they feel. I get it." Thomas said with genuine emotion and hurt. "They don't appreciate non ginneys! Not in the slightest!"

"Thomas!" Mary exclaimed, her voice shaking.

Thomas stood at the doorway of the dining room. Frustration was abundant in his expression. Anna and John looked at each other.

"They'll have to. Eventually." Emily responded back.

"Emily you stay out of this!" Anna reprimanded. Things were falling apart fast.

Gina, who had been quietly taking it all in, spoke for the first time at the dinner.

"See what you did! You knew Pop and mom wouldn't approve of this man. Yet you disobeyed and ruined what could have been a wonderful evening. I was looking forward to a nice meal with the Kaplan's, not with this man in our midst." She shot Thomas a quick glance.

"I suppose I need your approval too! This is unbelievable." Thomas snapped.

"Was that really appropriate to say?" Anna asked Gina.

"I really don't care if it's appropriate or not. It's the truth," Gina responded.

"Well, sometimes we don't always have to say what's on our mind. Especially when we're amongst friends," Anna kindly replied back. "Would you mind taking in the plates and start cleaning them for me?" She knew how to control Gina.

"Sure." She paused, then berated Mary with "How dare you!"

"Oh Gina, keep quiet!" Mary retorted.

Samuel put his hand over Gina's mouth.

"Gina pleasa, be quiet! Go insidea and clean!" He turned to Emily. "Youa saya bea Civil? I donta understand." Samuel asked innocently. His English was poor.

"Good, kind, nice. You understand now?" Emily explained to his blank face.

"I understand." Samuel nodded his head. "I donta like."

"We're aware of your disapproval. Trust me on that." Thomas yelled, while rolling his eyes. Under his breath, he muttered, "this is unbelievable." He sat back down.

Anna looked at Mary who had her head down. Then at Thomas who was getting more and more frustrated.

"So, how did you two meet?" John asked, as if totally oblivious to the situation. Anna gave him a quick nudge with her foot.

Mary looked down at her plate. Philomena banged on the table abruptly and excused herself.

There was a period of uncomfortable silence. Thomas coughed nervously. Neither Thomas nor Mary spoke a word.

"Paya noa attention. How youa meet?" Sam asked, shaking his head at his wife. She was in the other room.

As if this night could not get any worse, Philomena summoned Mary to the other room. The sound of her voice caused an uneasiness in the room. Anna looked at John who looked at

Samuel, who shrugged his shoulders. Mary kept her head down. A flood of tears was waiting to embark from her eyes. She had been trying to keep herself together the entire night.

"Marie! "Vieni qua." (*Come here*) Her mother's enraged voice gave her no chance to avoid it. The day Mary had feared came true. Why? Why in front of Tom? Her mind was drowning in emotions.

Mary knew she was in trouble. With tears of frustration coming down her face, she excused herself and followed her mother to the guest bedroom adjacent from the living room.

Her mother closed the door. She gestured for Mary to sit down on the swivel chair next to the queen-sized bed.

"Maria, Maria, perché sei comportato cosi stasera? Non avete idea di quanto dolore ci sei causato stasera. Abbiamo cercato di vedere un forte bello l'uomo italiano, non qualche l'uomo inglese da Indiana. Non siamo rischiato la nostra vita per venire qui dal vecchio mondo solamente per vedere che tu disobbedire alla tradizione.

Mia madre mi ha voluto sposare un italiano e lo fatto. Voglio che sia la mia figlia di sposare la nostra natura. Gli uomini italiani lavorano, supportano le loro famiglie. È questo che insegnano in questo collegio? Di disobbedire alla tua famiglia? Marca bene le mie parole Maria Sophia Mascia, non voglio alcuna menzione di questo Thomas Donahue in casa mia! Io sono quasi 60 anni e questo potrebbe uccidere il tuo padre ed io! Questo è quello che vuoi? Lui non è neanche un cattolico! Come sei mai pensati di sposarsi con qualcuno che non è nemmeno della nostra fede! Ti rinegherò dalla nostra famiglia sei vai davanti con questo!"

(*Maria, Maria, why are you doing this to us? You have no idea how much pain you have caused us tonight. We expected to see a strong, beautiful Italian man not some Englishman from Indiana. We did not risk our life to come here from the old world only for you to disobey the tradition.*)

(*My mother wanted me to marry an Italian and I did. I want it to be my daughters to marry our nature. Italian men are working hard, they provide for their families. Is this what they teach in this college? To disobey to your family? Mark my words Maria Sophia Mascia, I will not have any mention of this Thomas Donahue in my house! I am almost 60 years, and this could kill your father and me. Is this what you want? He is not even a Catholic! How dare you think to marry someone who is not even of our faith! I will disown you from family if you go through with this!*)

Philomena was out of breath. Her stone-cold face glared angrily at Mary, who just sat there. She knew it was a losing battle. Her parents would never approve of Tom. She also knew that Tom was her one true love. Philomena gestured for Mary to leave the room.

"Getta outta here!" She said under clenched teeth. Mary quietly walked back to the dining room. Everyone was silent. It was almost as if someone was shot. Tom and her father were nowhere to be seen.

This poor tortured soul. I have never seen her so happy in my life. Can't her parents see how confident she is around Tom Anna thought to herself before replying. "Tom is with your father in his garden."

Mary sighed heavily. "Oh, come on!"

Anna gave her a warm, comforting hug. "It's okay. I think it's best he and your father left. I don't think he needs to hear that kind of abuse."

Mary sobbed uncontrollably on Anna's shoulder. "I don't know what to do."

"Don't worry. All will work out." Anna said and continued to comfort her.

As a Jewish woman growing up in the early 20th century this brought back deep emotional pain that had been dormant in her mind. She had been through the emotional turmoil of cultural prejudice with her own family. It was her own personal emotional anguish that inspired her to develop a liberal mind. She would do her best to save Mary from an all too well-known pain that many immigrants felt.

The door to the dining room slowly creaked open. It was the silhouette of Philomena. She stood there not saying a word. Her eyes were red with anger.

With Mary's head buried in her shoulders crying hysterically, Anna made eye contact and mouthed the words, please leave.

Philomena nodded and left, slamming the front door on her way out.

Sam took Thomas for a long walk to his house. The ten-minute walk seemed like forever. Sam wouldn't say a word. What was going on Thomas wondered to himself.

The backyard was a true paradise. Thomas was greeted by apple trees, pear trees, peach trees, plumb trees, tomatoes, etc. It reminded Thomas of back home. This tiny backyard lot was full of every possible fruit tree one could imagine.

"This is absolutely beautiful! You have your own grocery store in your backyard," Thomas complimented Sam in the hopes of trying to win the old man's respect.

"You like?" Sam asked, taking a smoke from his pipe.

"Most certainly! It reminds me of back home."

"Glad youa like," his gravelly voice had softened up.

Sam took Thomas for a tour in his backyard. Pacing the yard slowly, as if in deep thought, Sam coughed his throat. He had a lot on his mind. He also knew this wouldn't be easy. He and Philomena knew what kind of man they wanted for their daughter. In fact, his wife wanted him to talk to him and let him know to back off.

Sam looked Thomas straight in the eyes. "You a good guy. You a smart. You a people person. I gotta no problem with you."

Thomas didn't buy a word of what he said.

"Except with me seeing your daughter," Thomas snapped, not afraid to show his feelings of hurt.

Sam shrugged his shoulders. "What you like in my daughter. Be honest." Sam bent down to check on his tomatoes. Satisfied, he stood up and looked at Tom.

"Sam, when I see your daughter, I see a beautiful soul. I see someone with the same drive, the same attitude as I. I see my potential wife."

"I see. You guys can be gooda friends. Marriage is no good. Won'ta work." He spit on the ground and shook his head.

Thomas shook his head. "That's insane. First off, this visit was not meant for me to come and ask for your daughter's hand in marriage. She wanted me to meet you so that I could know what kind of courtship I'm getting into. Secondly, it shouldn't matter what kind of culture a potential suitor is. What matters is how you love someone, how you can provide. I'm going to be a doctor soon. Financially, we will be all set. I just don't understand."

Sam put his hand on Tom's shoulder. "Understand this. We have no a need for you. No a good. No a good."

Sam looked down at the ground, shaking his head. "Won'ta work. No a good." He glared at Thomas, who was in a state of shock. The air was heavy with sadness and gloom.

A look of hurt came across Tom's face. Sam continued to look at him with a slight chance of remorse. This young man wanted to pursue his daughter. His wife dominated the house and in order to keep the peace, he had to do what she wanted. Sam secretly saw no problem with the man. He was good looking. The lack of money wasn't going to burden his daughter. They would be all set. The two would have numerous comforts he never had with his wife.

The old immigrant shook his head repeatedly. "My wife. She donta a like you. She and I have no a need for you. Whole thing no good."

"With all due respect you don't know me well enough to not like me. Mr Mascia, do you like me?" Thomas asked. squinting his eyes. They had both taken a seat on the old wooden bench Sam had made years prior.

Sam looked away, then coughed. "I think youa good man. My wife donta like. So youa gotta go. Gotta keep her happy." He shrugged his thin shoulders.

Thomas swallowed those words which hit every part of his body. We have no need for you. How despicable. How rude. If this were to be, what he wished it to be. How dare Mary obey her parents and their old school ways. This drive home would be a long one. He would have a word with her.

NINE

Modern Day

"I still remember the ride home that night. I cried myself to sleep that night." Mary recalled. She had just finished cooking the stuffed manicotti she bought at Costco. Her rule of thumb was that if you bought it at Costco, you can consider it homemade. The clock above her piano read 8:45 p.m. She and her guests were having an eventful evening. They were seated at her mahogany dining room table.

"This manicotti is out of this world!" Milagros said.

"Thank you. There is more in the kitchen. Help yourselves." Mary quietly had hoped that no one knew she didn't make it.

Milagros smiled and headed over to the kitchen. "Would anyone like some more?"

"This story is unbelievable. So, was that the last time you guys saw each other? What happened later that night?" Milagros had a thousand questions she wanted an answer to. She filled up her plate and sat back down.

"No, I would rebel against my parent's wishes and go on a four -day train ride to Indiana. As far as what happened that night. I would rather we not go there."

"What happened?" Milagros asked.

"I told you I would rather not speak about it." Mary snapped, while reaching for the box of Kleenex on the coffee table.

Thomas finished the last of his manicotti, then said, "There really isn't anything you haven't shared tonight. Why would this be any different?"

Mary knew she couldn't argue with reason.

She rolled her eyes. "Because it's painful too talk about but if you insist."

"No it's fine. We don't have to talk about it." Milagros spoke up.

Mary shrugged her shoulders. "I might as well talk about it. Let's just say I felt like I was ex-communicated from the family. That night my mother called Emily's apartment and scolded me to death. We spoke in Italian to each other. She said things like don't bother coming back home and you're such a disappointment to the family."

"I remember holding you in my arms that night trying to reassure you that everything is going to be okay," Thomas reached for the Kleenex. Tears of regret came down his aged face.

"You were wrong." Mary stated rather abruptly.

"Yes, I was wrong." Thomas painfully admitted. He sighed heavily.

"We both were." Mary said trying to fight the inevitable tears.

Mary stiffened her upper lip. She began to tear up. The emotional pain that had lay dormant for more than 60 years had been resurrected tonight. At 90 years of age, it was too much to think about. At the same time, it was therapeutic. This needed to happen.

"Wasn't he in Kansas?" Milagros inquired, trying to change the subject.

Thomas answered for Mary. "My family was in Indiana. My sister lived in Kansas, and that's where I resumed my studies. We had agreed to meet up in Indiana. My folks were both too elderly to travel long distance."

"Elderly? Look at us." Mary laughed.

"My dad passed away soon after your stay with us. While the rest of the world mourned the death of JFK, I was mourning the loss of my dear mom. She passed on the 22th of November 1963. She had often wished that Mary and I somehow got back together."

"Your folks were such good-hearted people. Everyone I met down there was so accepting of me," Mary reminisced.

Thomas nodded with a smile on his face.

"The difference between Connecticut and Indiana was like the difference between Oz and Kansas. No pun intended. The people down there were so kind and loving. They're all gone now. It's just Tom and I," Mary quietly stated.

Mary had a distant look in her eyes.

" I don't recall it being that bad. Though it certainly wasn't easy." Thomas softly spoke. "That's your version. My family was so supportive."

The old woman wiped away her tears.

"I remember it all too well. Anna tried her best to persuade them."

Mary sat still, looking off into the distance. "It's a memory that I wish would die off."

"I wanna know why. It doesn't make any sense," Milagros pleaded for answers.

"Old world thinking," Mary responded.

"Why? If they knew how happy you were? Why did they make such an issue?"

"Too many questions," Thomas quipped sipping his chardonnay.

"So that ended the relationship? I'm slightly confused," Milagros admitted. She took a sip of her Fresca, then put it down on the coffee table.

"It's complicated," Mary responded while taking her plate to the kitchen.

"That wasn't the last time. That was the last time I spoke to her family. They made it clear that they wanted no part of me in their life." Thomas shrugged his shoulders. "What can you do. Maybe it was best."

"Yeah, but why?" Milagros asked hoping to make sense of the injustice. These two would have been perfect for each other. She took a bite of her manicotti and patiently listened to Mary's response.

Mary had come back from the kitchen and slowly sat back down on her love seat.

"Because I was the tradition breaker. I went to college, would've married a successful doctor. Who knows, maybe we would have moved away. Back in those days, traveling wasn't as easy as it is today. So, the chance of me seeing my family again was slim to none. Who knows?"

"Why would it have been best that it didn't work out?" Milagros asked.

Thomas gave a deep sigh. "Are you married?"

Milagros shook her head no.

"When you marry someone, you don't just marry that person. You marry their family as well. So whatever problems they have you inherit. It wouldn't have done us good to have that kind of hatred in the family." Thomas took a bite of his food and looked up at Mary. "Such a beautiful life together we could've had."

Milagros asked Thomas, "What about your family? Were they opposed?"

"We just told you how loving and supportive his family was. Don't you remember?" Mary interrupted.

"In most stories, it's the opposite. The wealthy family looks down on the poor. Your story seems to be the opposite. Romeo and Juliette, Thomas and Mary," Milagros said, joking in the end.

"This isn't some made up love story. This really happened young lady!" Mary proclaimed.

Milagros began to apologize but was cut off by Tom.

"Romeo and Juliette took the easy way out. I endured that pain for many years." Thomas spoke with genuine frustration.

Mary sighed deeply.

Thomas cleared his throat. "Can I please answer her question?"

"Go ahead." Both women answered in unison.

Thomas spoke his words slowly. "No. They loved her. My family truly loved Mary. Which is what made it worse. If they had opposed too, then then our breakup wouldn't have been so bad. They wanted us to fight. They knew we were made for each other."

Thomas reached for the Kleenex on Mary's coffee table.

"Your family were such nice people. Your mother was a real sweetheart. The farthest trip I ever took was to Indiana to meet your family. I remember it like it was yesterday. Didn't you have a maid? What was her name again?"

"Nellie. She was such a dear old woman." Thomas replied.

"She was like a Grandmother to me." Mary reminisced.

"To us. You mean." Thomas smiled warmly.

Mary had a dreamy look in her eyes. A distant look. Thomas was right; if it weren't for her family's traditions, if it weren't for the lack of understanding on her parent's part, this elderly man would have been her husband of almost 70 years. They would have had a beautiful life together. There would be problems, but she would feel at ease with him as her protector.

"Yes they were good people. It's nice to hear you say that. We never really talked about how we felt. This whole experience is therapeutic. It took us 70 years to communicate but we did."

Thomas gave Mary a warm smile. Mary looked at him and nodded. "God made sure we made amends. I really do believe that."

Higher education had encouraged him to question the existence of God whereas life had reassured him that God was very much alive. After some hesitation Thomas nodded his head. "Indeed he did."

Thomas turned his attention to Milagros. "I believe it's now my turn to speak." Milagros sat back. This was going to be good.

TEN

(Thomas' Story)

Certain people fit the mold of Noblesville, Indiana. You had the sons of farmers who wore straw hats with dirty overalls, chewed tobacco, and worked from sunrise to sunset. These young men knew nothing of the world around them but knew everything about the earth. And then you had the upper class, educated young men who were academic scholars but knew nothing about life. Thomas Donahue never fit in with either. He was very much ahead of his time. He never related with the privileged class of young men whom he had grown up around. Young men whose fathers were very well to do but who themselves had no substance.

Every Thursday, his father would drive to town in his 1938 Phantom Corsair, which he took great pride in, to discuss the politics of the day with old men who were, in Thomas's mind, parrots that repeated what their professors taught them some 50 years prior. One thing about his dad that he did admire was that, while he was well to do, he wasn't an arrogant snob. Thomas always thought in the back of his mind that deep down his dad was just a regular guy trying to play a role he was given.

Thomas would go along with his father and sit in the smoke-filled rooms with the velvet arm chairs and listen to old men give their outdated views on life. The club was called The Beaumont. Only the well to do could qualify for a membership. Thomas was determined in his mind to not let whatever status he acquired mold him.

"Huck, do you ever feel like you're stuck in a rut?" Thomas asked, picking a red delicious apple from the Baden Farm trees. Baden Farms was a well-established farm in the area that had over two hundred acres of land. You could pick strawberries, blueberries, pears and apples during the season. You would pick your fill and then have it weighed by Mr. Baden on his scale that sat in the front of his general store. It was 92 cents a pound now. It had gone up twenty cents in the past year.

Huck Bradbury was one of Thomas's closest friends. They had gone to school together. Huck was a down to earth, son of a farmer type guy. He had dirty blonde hair and enthusiastic blue eyes.

"As in?" asked Huck taking out a rotten apple from his basket.

Thomas sighed, "As in, you don't fit in. As in, everything you do is decided for you. Do you believe in fate?" Thomas asked, sincerely troubled. Huck's father was the local pastor at the church. Thomas knew he would always get the right answer from Huck.

Not necessarily the answer he wanted to hear. But, the right answer. The one that required taking the pill of truth, swallowed by a dose of humility.

"You know God created us with free will. He doesn't make the decisions for you. He also isn't to blame for all the wrong. If you're that unhappy with your life, you can always change. We are both young guys. We don't have to live our father's lives. You think I wanna spend my life plowing fields?" Huck laughed. "The heck with that. I've heard California is nice. I wouldn't mind living out there. Truthfully pal, Indiana just isn't for me." He felt a sense of relief.

"It's just so frustrating. You are a Donahue. You go to college, get married, make money. I'm more about the simple life. People are so worried about titles in my family. It's ridiculous. I mean I'm gonna pursue my Ph.D. because that's what Donahue men do," Thomas said, shaking his head in frustration.

"Remember these three words, man. It's YOUR LIFE! You can't live your life trying to please everyone. In the end, you'll be miserable. I always believed that was the root cause of depression. I just don't have any degree to prove it," Huck said with a smile on his face. They have had this conversation before when Thomas had been accepted to Yale.

"You, my friend, have something more valuable than a degree. You have good old-fashioned horse sense. I've read

Freud, and honestly, he's a quack. I learn more from you about life. Then any of these so-called intellectuals."

Huck grinned. "A lot of it comes from a dusty old book that hasn't been used in God knows how long. It just sits there in your father's study, collecting dust." The Donahue's claimed to be devout Christians. Their definition of devout meant coming for Christmas Eve mass and the occasional Sunday 9 a.m. service, which hadn't been the case for a good six months.

"I know. I've been slacking. Right now, I have no time for religion."

"You can't set aside an hour a week for God? After all that he's blessed you with?" Huck looked at him with concern. This idea of higher learning ruined him.

Thomas gave it a thought. "I don't want a sermon."

"Well, you need to make time for God," exclaimed Huck, as he examined the contents to of his basket. "You done?"

"I guess we should call it a day," Thomas said, holding a basket of apples up to his chest.

The two men walked toward the general store located at the bottom of the hill.

The inside of the store was as old as the farm itself. The floorboards creaked with every step you took. The father of the two Baden boys worked the store. The old man weighed the apples. "That will be $1.67."

Huck handed him the money and proceeded out the door while Tom was still in line with a bar of chocolate fudge.

"That will be 4.60," The elderly farmer said, taking the burlap bag of chicken feed off the counter. Inside the tiny store was homemade, mile-high apple pies, homemade soaps, and numerous kinds of candy along with Coca-Cola.

"You keep going up in price. You think we have money to waste."

A large woman with her hair pulled back tight and two kids in toe remarked. "Next year, I wouldn't be surprised if it was 7 dollars a bag. I can't afford that. You're the only place for miles that has the kind of feed my chickens eat."

"Maybe it's best you buy your feed elsewhere. I'm not to blame for the high prices," said 87-year-old Henry Baden who was getting sick and tired of dealing with the struggling few of Noblesville.

"Perhaps I will. You know full well my family is having a hard time. We've been loyal customers for years."

"There is nothing I can do about it. Everything has gone up. I just filled up my truck and it cost me $1.80. I remember when 50 cents would fill me up."

Henry saw the suffering in the woman's expression. She had just lost her husband in the war and had three children to look after. Everyone knew everyone's else's struggles. It was a very close-knit town.

"I know it's not your fault. Can't you lower the price? It's late in the hour and I've got to go home and feed the chickens."

"Lady, you're getting on my nerves! Either you pay or you leave!"

"How much does she owe?" asked Thomas.

"Oh no. You don't have to pay." The woman was clearly embarrassed.

"4.60," the old man answered.

"Can you pay 2 dollars?" Thomas asked the woman.

"Yes, I can pay 2 dollars." She took out her purse and took out two single dollar bills.

"The price is $4.60. That's final," the old man snapped.

"Have her give you her 2 dollars and I'll pitch in the 2.60."

The woman was beyond grateful. She gave Thomas a hug. "God bless you son. I just barely could afford my rent, never mind pay 4.60 for feed."

"I'm glad I could help. If you're ever able to help someone else, do it. Pass it on."

The large woman laughed. "Will do."

There was a bitterness that covered over the town like a poisonous gas. People were struggling. People were angry. And then you had the Donahue's ...

ELEVEN

70-year-old Frank Donahue lived what many would call a good life. He and his wife, Margret, who was an American studying abroad when they met and married in 1901, lived in a comfortable home in the outskirts of town. Money was all Frank knew. He was a retired surgeon and a good one at that. Two of his boys were sent through the loop. They focused on their education, got married, had kids and created a life of their own. The oldest, Chester, was a clinical psychologist. He and his family lived in Seattle. Then there was Douglas, he was an optometrist who made Baltimore his home. He had a daughter, Rachel, who lived in Kansas.

Finally, there was Thomas. He was the youngest of the boys. While he still lived at home, Thomas was a driven young man. Frank just wished he would settle down and get married. Someday Frank thought. Someday he would get married. His health was poor. Diabetes had slowed him down. He wasn't the same Frank Donahue that he was just a few years prior. The one thing Frank hated, money could not protect him from—the ravages of old age. He had thick white hair and wore dark, coke-bottle shaped glasses.

"Any good news today?" asked Nellie Fairbanks, the family's live-in maid. Nellie was an elderly woman of Irish descent, who was of short stature and slight in build. For the past 20 years she was the family's cook and maid. "I don't expect there is," continued Nellie, answering her own question. Just then the family's 10-year-old sheep dog named Teddy came in the kitchen.

Frank sat down in the kitchen with the Noblesville Newsworthy paper in his hands. "The same old nonsense. The war is still going on. I doubt I will live to see the end of it. By the way, this French toast is excellent, job well done. Teddy down!" The affectionate dog tried to grab at Frank's food.

"Come here, Teddy, come on." The dog obediently followed Nellie. She led the dog to the other room and closed the door. After a few minutes of barking, the dog laid down to sleep.

"The poor thing is getting old." Nellie noticed. Arthritis had crippled his back leg. "I remember him as a young pup."

"Aren't we all. I remember when I had my health," Frank quipped.

"You know, the other day I was thinking. What was the purpose of World War I? Some half-drunk took a shot and killed the arch duke and somehow that caused everyone to give a damn and go after each other? I still remember how peaceful the spring of 1914 was. Those days are long past gone. I often wonder what the next twenty or thirty years will bring. America isn't the same as it was when we arrived in November of 19."

Frank put the paper down, sipped his coffee as the grandfather clock in the hallway rang. It was 9 a.m. on a gloomy cloudy day.

"You're feeling rather philosophical today, Mr. Donahue." Nellie smiled while cleaning the dishes.

Frank chuckled. "I remember when my father would talk about the good old days when he was old. It always annoyed me. I would always remind him that the 1850's weren't so great. Men were lucky to live past 60. Women died during childbirth. The factory that he worked at was downright disgusting. He would smile and say that was all he knew. And at the time, things weren't as bad as they are now. I suppose I'm turning into my old man. Oh, and Nellie you know better than to call me Mr. Donahue. Marge and I view you as an old friend. In many ways, you're like an aunt to Thomas."

Nellie had been worried about the young man who had seemed a little distant in the past couple of months. Her own son died during childbirth, so the Donahue boys were like her own kids. She used the opportunity to bring up her concern. "I always viewed your boys as nephews of my own. I was just wondering ... is Thomas okay? He just seems so forlorn. He needs a good wife."

"I think a woman is the last thing on his mind." Frank ate the last of his french toast. "Personally, Margret and I would love to see him settle down and find a wife."

"Well, why doesn't he? He's a handsome young man." Nellie took a seat at the table and started eating her own breakfast.

Frank shook his head. "His mind is always preoccupied with something. Now he's focusing on his studies." Frank explained, putting his suit jacket on. "I'm off to The Beaumont. Thomas is supposed to be home soon. He gave his word he would meet me there. Marge is out playing pinochle with her lady friends. I'll see you later."

"Oh, Frank, you're forgetting something. It's the second Friday of the month." Nellie gently reminded him.

"Oh, yes. You're right. It's payday for you." He reached for his wallet and took out a crisp 50-dollar bill and handed it to her. As a live-in maid, her expenses where kept to a bare minimum. She received free room and board if her health allowed her to work.

Nellie took the money and put it in her pocket. She was paid 50 dollars every two weeks to cook and clean for the family. It usually took her a good day to clean and tidy up the six-bedroom, three-bathroom family home. At 79, her health was good. That's what she told them. Truth be told, it was getting harder and harder for her to keep up with the ever-demanding duties. While she thought about retiring and going her own way, the sad truth was that the world no longer had any use for an old widow such as herself. She was still, however, very much of use to the Donahue family. That's why she will work till she can't. In a cruel unforgiving world that shunned the poor and the elderly, the Donahue family was her only hope. Nellie never forgot that.

TWELVE

Thomas opened the mahogany door to his family's house. He and Huck had brought home four baskets full of Granny Smith and Red Delicious apples. Huck helped him bring in the last basket.

"I'll see you at the diner in 45 minutes, gotta run home and change out of these overalls. I want to look nice when meeting your lady."

Thomas thanked Huck, who closed the door and took off for home. His day had started at 5 a.m. and didn't end till sunset.

"Are you forgetting something son?" Frank asked coming down the stairs.

Normally, every Thursday he and his father went to The Beaumont. An old aging building with old well-to-do men who talked about politics while drinking cheap brandy. Thomas secretly had a strong disdain for it.

"I ... uh ... You see I met this girl several months back from Connecticut and we bonded. She's gonna stay down here for two weeks. She wants to meet the family."

Frank was stunned. "A girl? Coming tonight?"

"Well Dad ... I uh was going to tell you. Mom and Nellie knew about it. I figured eventually I would let you know," Thomas spoke in a timid manner.

Frank laughed. "Eventually, you would tell me." He smiled to himself before going on. "Well son, it's about time you settled down and find a girl. Do I know her family? Are you engaged to be?"

"No. Not yet. There are some complications that must be worked out. Her name is Mary. Mary Mascia." Thomas was hesitant about going into the cultural shock her parents had.

"Mascia? Sounds Italian." Frank shrugged his shoulders.

"She is, dad, she's an Italian immigrant. I mean, she's really the daughter of Italian immigrants, I mean she was born there but…" his father, sensing his pain, interrupted

"No, son, it's okay. If you brought home a colored girl, it still wouldn't be an issue. Your mother and I are more than happy to have whomever you choose to be our daughter-in-law. But son ..." Frank looked at the floor, then at his son.

"Dad, I know where this is going," Thomas sighed.

Neither one of them spoke.

Frank was genuinely concerned for his son. Something didn't seem right. There shouldn't be any complications when courting a young lady.

"Complications? Well, what sort of complications? Is she poor? Not that it matters," Frank asked.

Thomas was taken aback by his father's bluntness. "Like I said, she's the daughter of two Italian immigrants. Dad, I really don't wanna talk about it. Huck and I were gonna grab a bite at the diner before we pick her up."

"Son, I really think we should talk about ..." he was cut off by an overjoyed Nellie.

"A young lady is coming over here tonight? Did I hear that correctly? This calls for a celebration!"

"Didn't my mother tell you?" Thomas kindly reminded the elderly woman.

"I'm afraid she did. You'll have to forgive this old geezer." Nellie laughed at her mistake. "80 is around the corner, and my mind isn't as sharp as it once was."

"We don't have any old geezers around here," Frank warmly replied. "Unless you include me." He gave a friendly wink at the old maid.

The three of them laughed in unison.

Nellie blushed. "You're too kind. I suppose I better get started on tonight's banquet."

"I'm sure we will be in for a delightful surprise dinner tonight." Frank said with every ounce of genuine praise.

Thomas smiled. Nellie, along with his folks, was getting older. Mary and he would take care of them in the years to come, he thought to himself. Nellie was in her late 70s and she had slowed down considerably in the last year. She was more like a grandma then a maid.

After giving Nellie a hug, Thomas said, "I figured we could have a nice hot apple pie for desert tonight. Huck and I went picking this morning."

"Sounds good. I'll run to the general store and pick up a few things. I can't wait to meet her." Nellie could hardly contain herself.

"Her train comes in at 5 p.m. We probably won't get home till 5:30 or so."

"It's a good 45 minutes to Indianapolis. I don't think you two will be home till at least 6:30, give or take the traffic." Frank mentioned.

"You're right," Thomas responded.

"I'll have the food ready by 7. Take care, kiddo." Nellie gave Thomas a warm, grandmotherly hug. She then took her coat out of the hallway closet and headed out the front door. It was just Thomas and his worried father.

"Son is everything okay?" Frank inquired Thomas was very much to himself. Something was off.

"Dad. Please, I'll be fine." Thomas insisted.

Frank cleared his throat. "I have to be honest. Your mom and I haven't been good examples in attending church services. I can't think of the last sermon we went to. Nonetheless, we are a Christian household. This young lady is more than welcome to visit our family. If your living in my house, she will be staying in her own room. You know how we feel."

"That's fine. You'll see she's a very respectful young lady." Thomas replied.

Frank put his frail hand on Thomas's broad shoulder.

Frank chuckled. "I look forward to meeting her. I trust your judgment. I must get going. I'll see you and the next Mrs. Donahue at 7 p.m."

"See you then," Thomas responded. He couldn't help but smile at the thought of Mary being his future wife.

Frank was on his way out the front door when he turned around.

"Thomas?"

Thomas turned around, he was headed to the kitchen.

"Yes?"

"Just for curiosity sake. What is the problem? Is it the long distance? Your mother did notice a ton of letters from a young lady in Connecticut. Is that the issue?"

"No." Thomas slowly paused. "No, it's not. It's her parents."

"Her parents?" Frank looked bewildered. His son was tall, handsome, intelligent, and going to be a doctor. What could her parents possibly have against him?

Thomas spoke slow and quiet. "They don't approve of us being together simply because I'm not Italian."

"Not Italian? Thomas, you're going to be a doctor. I can understand if she came from colored folk. Society hasn't been very accepting of us white folk marrying the colored. One day, I'm sure it will change. You know how your mother and I feel about racial equality."

"Dad. I have to go."

Frank looked at his son and slowly replied, "Enjoy your lunch. Don't let someone's ignorance ruin a beautiful opportunity. This is America. Land of the free. You're free to marry whomever you want. Remember that son."

Thomas smiled. "Thanks Dad. I needed that."

Frank looked at his son straight in the eye. "Never forget where you're from. This is Noblesville. Remember that."

Tom looked at his father and after a brief pause, said, "Thanks. I really appreciate it."

"You know what I mean?" Frank asked, making sure he got the point.

"Yes. Yes, I do." Thomas gave his father a reassuring smile. He then said goodbye and continued his way.

Thomas knew the history of his town was founded by a mixed-race couple. The founder of Noblesville was a white man by the name of William Conner. He was married to a native American woman by the name of Mekinges, the daughter of Indian chief Kikthawenund. She was Indian royalty who had great influence on Conner's trading post business. Their relationship earned him the trust and business of fellow native Americans. If a white man could earn the trust of his fellow native, there was no doubt in Tom's mind that he could earn the trust and respect of Samuel and Philomena Mascia.

Norman's Diner was a small, bustling place that served great food at a reasonable price. As the usual, there was a long wait at the door. The smell of cigarette smoke greeted Thomas as he opened the door. Huck had gotten there earlier and gotten

A LETTER FROM *Thomas*

a booth by the counter. The juke box was playing some type of jazz music.

"What will it be fellas?" asked the young peppy waiter.

"I'll have the blue plate special. And a cup of coffee. Two creams and one teaspoon of sugar," said Huck, placing his menu on the table.

"And you, sir?" The waiter asked Thomas.

"I'll have an ice cream soda. Extra scoop of vanilla."

"Are you sure you don't want something more substantial? We have a great fried chicken dinner for .65 cents. It comes with mashed potatoes and fresh corn. Also, we throw in a hot bun. Made from scratch."

"Nah, no thanks. I'm not too hungry."

"It will be an additional .10 cents for the extra scoop."

"That's fine." Thomas gave the waiter his menu. He had his head down, lost in a fog.

"Are you okay? You seem a little distant," Huck said sipping his water.

Thomas raised his head up slowly. He had bags under his eyes.

"A few months ago, when I met her folks it was a complete disaster. I love Mary, I truly do. I just." He paused to get his thoughts together. "I'm worried."

"Worried bout what?" Huck asked wiping up some water that had spilled with his napkin.

"Will my parents approve of her? Will she like the town of Noblesville? Will her folks ever get rid of this irrational fear of their daughter marrying a non-Italian? If she and I have kids will her folks take out their anger on them?"

Huck listened to his friend. "I think you're jumping the gun. Just a bit. Are you sure that she's the one? How long have you known her for?"

"I thought you supported my relationship with her? If you don't feel she's the one, then be honest. I can't take this subliminal talk."

"It's not my decision to make. I'm just trying to get you to think clearly. I want you to be happy and content," Huck said, wiping the ketchup from his chin.

Thomas nodded his head.

Huck always had the right kind of questions. Thomas knew in his heart that she was the one. He had never had this kind of emotional attachment to anyone. Every single day, all he thought about was Mary. How was she doing? Was she happy? The young lady he met that memorable night was his obsession.

"I have courted several women over the years. Mary is different. All I ever think about is her. Every other day, I'm writing letters to her. She has a beautiful, intelligent mind. I can't explain my feelings for her."

"It sounds like you have a strong infatuation for her." Huck had summoned the waiter for more water. The waiter poured his glass and tended to the other patrons.

"No, no you're wrong. This isn't some teenage relationship that begins and ends in a month. This love is real. It's amazing how true love feels." Thomas had a far-away look in his eyes.

"As long as I've known you, you've always been one to take your time. You're a very methodical man. Let me ask you, do you think you can put up with her parent's ignorance?"

Thomas shook his head. "No marriage is perfect. You remember when my folks temporarily split up in the summer of '34? That was the worst two years of my life. My sister is still scared from the things my old man had said and done. You ever wonder why she's all alone in Kansas? But my folks got through it and they are stronger than ever now."

"True, but they didn't have that kind of hatred from the in-laws. I mean they didn't start off on thin ice. Marriage is tough for everyone. Some things are harder to deal with than others." Huck tried to reason with Thomas, but he kept avoiding the truth.

"Doesn't it say that marriage 'is a trouble in the flesh'? In the Bible? You're the preacher. Not me," Thomas asked, taking a sip from his ice cream soda.

Huck took a bite of his corn beef hash. "Yes. Yes, it does. Their reaction isn't a normal reaction. They will never support you and Mary. I'm not saying don't pursue her. It's just, you've got to be smart. What exactly did her folks say?"

"I would rather not go back to that nightmare," Thomas said wiping his face with a napkin.

Huck wasn't buying it. "If you two get serious, you're gonna have to face 'that nightmare' again and again."

Thomas shrugged his shoulders. "Her folks spoke in broken English. They were very hard to understand. Basically, they do not want their daughter married to an Englishman. They made it very clear."

"I'm sure it was just a language barrier. That's all." Huck was optimistic.

"I understand where you're coming from but it's not a language issue. It's a cultural issue."

Huck was slowly eating his food. He was trying to discern whether Thomas was overly sensitive. "I'm sure you're mistaken. It doesn't seem at all rational."

"I'm not crazy," Thomas said with a touch of sadness.

"Never said you were. You were the one who suggested that, not me." Huck had finished his meal and ordered a slice of chocolate cake.

"I'm not mistaken, and they aren't being rational. When we got back to Mary's friend's place, her mother called her up and berated her to death in Italian. None of us knew what she was saying. Judging by the tears pouring down Mary's face, we knew it wasn't good. She hung up the phone and just cried her eyes out."

"Well, we can't change the past; I promise you, we will change the future. Your family is very loving, and I only see your relationship getting stronger down here. You have all the support in the world down here in Noblesville. Who knows, maybe I'll be the one to marry you guys."

"Without a doubt. I don't know how my family will receive her. Honestly, I'm a little nervous. "

"Your parents are educated and with education, comes understanding. I'm sure all will be well. Put it in God's hands."

Huck finished the last of his cake. "Well, it's time we head out and pick up your girl." The two men stood up and made their way to the front and as usual, Huck treated.

"She won't mind being picked up in my old jalopy?" Huck asked, pulling out of the busy driveway.

"Not at all. She's not that type. The mechanic said my car should be ready by tomorrow. They had to order a part from the next town over."

Huck laughed. "I'm glad. Don't let what happened in New Haven get you down. The Midwest is a whole different crew of people."

"How can I not forget what they did to me?" Thomas replied.

"Don't give people the power to control you. Things will work themselves out. Just give it time, and let God take care of it."

"You know, you're a true friend. I appreciate your candidness. I'm gonna catch some shut eye." Thomas closed his eyes and dozed off.

They arrived at Indianapolis Union station roughly at a quarter past 6. Parents were picking up their children. Young men were saying their final goodbyes to their wives. Amongst the crowd stood a very shy young woman with a nervous expression on her face. Her face lit up when she saw the old beat up truck with her lover exiting out of the passenger seat. The two embraced each other and exchanged kisses. Thomas took her luggage and gently placed it in the cab of the truck. Once she was settled in, Huck slowly drove off. Neither one of them could have imagined how beautiful life would be in Noblesville, Indiana.

THIRTEEN

"I'm sure she's a lovely woman," Marge spoke while touching up her curly reddish hair. She and her husband were in their master bedroom finishing up getting ready for tonight's dinner with Mary. Frank was looking in the mirror, buttoning up his white dress shirt. His mind was flooded with unanswered questions.

Marge was the matriarch of the Donahue family. She was known in town for her outspoken charismatic personality. Marge loved everybody and everybody loved her. She felt at ease now that her son was in a serious relationship.

"A lovely woman with complications," Frank added trying to finish tying his tie. His wife fixed his back collar which was up. "I don't know what to make of it. That's the word our son specifically used, complications."

"Our son wasn't given a fair chance. As a mother, it disturbs me. I refuse to do the same to this poor girl. She deserves all our love and support. Please do not give her any problems."

"Why does it disturb you?" Frank asked out of curiosity.

"You mean to tell me it doesn't disturb you?" Marge was taken aback.

"Not in the very least. I think disturb is too strong of a word. I'm more perplexed." Frank shook his head and coughed.

"Disturbed is the perfect word," Marge said with a sense of confidence.

Marge turned to Frank and looked him directly in the eyes.

"You know what kind of man our son is. You know what kind of provider he will be. The fact that someone would judge him based on what part of the pond he's from is downright insane. When it's your son, it's personal."

"We forget that cultural discrimination isn't just a colored verses white dilemma. Honestly, I never thought our own son would feel the pain of discrimination. It didn't seem like such a bother where I grew up in England."

"Cultural discrimination is definitely an issue in America. I don't want to talk about it. Please do not bring it up over dinner. The time is not yet to talk about it."

"Now, why would I do that? If she really is the wonderful person that he says she is, then she will have our backing." Frank smiled.

"Our son deserves the best. It would be foolish on our part to allow old-world bigotry destroy something as beautiful as marriage." Frank continued his thought.

"Which is why this has to be resolved." Marge sighed.

"It will be. Don't you worry about it." Frank assured.

"It's just so upsetting." She was cut off by the sound of footsteps walking toward the door.

There was a slight knock at the bedroom door. Frank opened the door to reveal a worn-out Nellie. She had been cooking all day and making sure the place was pristine for their guest.

"They just pulled in the driveway. The table is set and ready," Nellie said with enthusiasm.

"Thank you, Nellie. The place looks like we're gonna expect the President and the First Lady tonight." Marge complimented.

Nellie blushed. "Thank you." She had always appreciated a genuine compliment.

"Is the guest bedroom ready for Mary? I'm sure she's gonna wanna wash up before we eat." Frank added.

Nellie nodded. "All is well. Now come downstairs and meet your future daughter in law."

Frank looked at Marge and she looked at him. This would be a night to cherish. The elderly couple had waited many years for this night to come.

FOURTEEN

"Nellie, please put the dog in the basement for the night," Frank ordered. The goofy sheepdog had tried to give Mary a lick on the face. Huck had just finished bringing in the last of her belongings. It had rained steadily throughout the afternoon. Thomas gave Mary a brief tour of the city. She saw the rundown parts as well as the nicer part of town. People seemed content in Noblesville. They seemed happy despite not having much.

Frank extended his hand to the young woman who seemed to be at home. She had a beautiful radiance about her. This gorgeous young lady would be my future daughter-in-law, Frank thought to himself.

He gave her a sincere smile. "My name is Frank. I've heard so much about you. Welcome to the family. Please make yourself at home."

Mary smiled. "Oh, it's a pleasure to meet you. I'm Mary. Mary Mascia is my full name. I've waited so long to meet you all, I just can't believe the day has come."

"We've been eagerly awaiting your arrival," Frank spoke with genuine happiness.

A heavy-set woman with red curly hair wearing a blue dress with turquoise earrings stepped forward.

"I'm Marge." The large woman gave Mary a warm, comforting hug. "You are more beautiful than I expected."

Mary blushed. "Thank you. You're all so kind."

The kitchen door opened, and Nellie stepped out and into the main hallway.

"I'm Nellie. I'm the maid. If there is anything, I can do to make your stay more enjoyable, please don't hesitate to ask. Thomas has told me a lot about you." The elderly woman gave Mary a firm hug. "Welcome to the family."

"Would you like to freshen up before dinner?" Marge asked. "You must be exhausted."

"No. I haven't eaten since this morning," Mary replied truthfully.

She took off her jacket and hung it up in the front closet.

"Since this morning? You must be starved." Marge said in a concerned motherly tone.

"I was just so nervous, I suppose my nerves got the best of me." Mary felt foolish for admitting her feelings.

Marge understood her feelings.

"Sweetheart, you have absolutely nothing to be nervous about. You're one of the family."

"Did he tell you how he was treated?" Mary asked. She then repeated herself. "Did he?"

"You aren't in New Haven anymore. You're in Noblesville, Indiana. We welcome people, we don't reject them. Whatever happened back home, stays at home. Understand?" Marge said, while her eyes comforted Mary's eyes.

Thomas did not want any mention of Connecticut or her parents in his house. He decided to change the subject.

"You're in for some good old-fashioned country food," Thomas said, gesturing for Huck to bring her bags up to her room. "It's the 4th bedroom on the right."

Huck took her bags and walked up the stairs.

"You have such a beautiful house." Mary exclaimed to Frank. "It has such character and charm. Quite lovely."

"Thank you. We like it. Let me show you to the dining room."

"Thomas, why don't you show your girl to the dining room. I have to run down to the cellar and bring up some wine."

"My pleasure. Mary, please follow me," he said as he gently took her hand.

Thomas ushered her to the large dining room. Frank sat at the head of the table. Mary and Thomas sat next to each other. Nellie poured everyone some water.

Marge and Nellie were bringing in the food. Two large plates of roasted chicken and honey baked ham, along with fresh corn and mashed potatoes. Marge brought out a plate with hot dinner rolls. Everything looked and smelled delicious.

"I never knew I was coming to a feast. Thank you all so much. This is quite lovely. I'm really touched." Mary smiled.

"Our pleasure. So, how exactly did you two meet? I wanna hear both stories tonight." Marge asked, taking a sip of her water.

"Mom." Thomas answered a tad embarrassed.

"You two are in a courtship. It's a harmless question." Marge said, helping herself to the freshly chucked yellow corn.

"It's okay, Tom. I don't mind." Mary chuckled nervously.

"You knew the question was going to come up. Better sooner than later," Nellie said, helping herself to another homemade bun.

"No its fine." Mary turned to Thomas. "How did we meet? It seems so long ago."

Thomas laughed. "It was only eight months ago. We met at a party in Port Washington and enjoyed some horseback riding the next day. Now, I don't want to sound cliché, but it was love at first sight."

"Maybe for you." Mary responded with a big goofy smile on her face. "I thought you were a nut at first. I remember nothing of that night except for our conversation. My initial judgement of you was wrong."

"Thank heavens your first impression was wrong." Thomas chuckled.

Mary laughed. She felt comfortable around the Donahues. Almost as if they were family. Long lost family.

"You guys are going to make such a cute couple." Nellie said with a grin on her wrinkled face.

Mary blushed three shades of pink.

The table laughed. "So, you're at Yale I take it?" Frank asked Mary.

"Columbia. I started off at the New Haven Teachers college. I'm going for my masters at Columbia"

"Impressive. It's not everyone who gets accepted to Columbia. Clearly, you're an intelligent woman." Frank sat up in his chair. He was finding himself to be fond of her. It was only an hour since they met, but he felt like she was already part of the family.

Mary shrugged. "I wouldn't say I'm any smarter than the next person. I just have a greater appreciation for learning than most."

"Do you think that has something to do with being an immigrant? Or I should say the daughter of an immigrant couple? It's just something I've always wondered." Marge asked innocently.

Mary gave it some thought. "Oh, absolutely! I think we are more driven to succeed then most. Society tells us that if you want to succeed in life, then you must get yourself a degree. For those of us who aren't native to America, it's even more important to have a proper education."

"Society isn't always correct my dear. Many years ago, society said a woman couldn't vote. It wasn't terribly long ago when we got our chance," Nellie stated in a grandmotherly tone.

"I have to disagree on that one. My father left school during the 5th grade to help his family out. He's doing quite well for himself. We have one of the biggest farms in Indiana." Huck spoke up.

"From my perspective, education is very important. America isn't all that welcoming to foreigners." Mary said sipping her water. "That's a myth that attracted many people to America over the decades."

"It is true. Sadly, your correct." Frank took a bite of his food.

"Would you feel the same way if your family was American?" Thomas asked out of curiosity.

Mary looked down at her plate, then slowly raised her head up. "No, I don't think I would. But then one may never know."

Frank cleared his throat. "Although a college education is important, it certainly isn't for everyone. I think the point Mary is trying to make is that a proper education would give an immigrant the respect they deserve. To Huck's point, there are plenty of people in this world who do well for themselves without a college degree."

Everyone nodded in unison

"I never stepped foot in a place of higher learning. Life and all its lessons taught me more than any degree." Nellie replied while cutting up her chicken.

"Good point." Thomas said quietly under his breathe.

"I was born in the U.S. and we take so much for granted." Marge responded. "I never can really say I understand your dilemma. My parents were poor, but we were American. It makes a difference."

"So, you're a teacher?" Huck asked cutting himself some of the ham.

"On my way to be." Mary softly smiled.

"What type of teacher?" Huck asked.

"Kindergarten thru third grade."

Frank sat up in his chair. "Why in particular? Just out of curiosity sake? You're obviously a very accomplished woman. Why teaching?"

Mary gave it some thought. "Young children are the future of America. They have a special innocence about them. It's hard to say why exactly."

"If it wasn't for good teachers like yourself, the world would not have these fine bright young people defending us against the enemy." Frank stated.

Mary wasn't one to talk about herself. Trying to change the subject, she turned to Nellie and asked, "How long have you worked for the Donahues?"

Nellie sat up in her chair and wiped her face with a handkerchief. "I've known them for many years. It's been about twenty years or so. They came at the right time in my life."

"How so?" Mary wondered.

"I would rather not go into it. All I'll say is that they are like dear family to me. It really warms my heart to know that Thomas found someone like you."

"Oh, Nellie," Thomas said, rather surprised at her reaction.

"It's the truth. You have yourself a lovely compliment of a woman." Nellie smiled at Mary.

"That's very sweet of you. It's getting late, I should get going now." Mary nervously said, trying to fight back tears. Sometimes in life you meet people that are so sincere and genuine. The Donahues were such people. It warmed her heart to know that she would be part of such a wonderful family. Thomas and I would prevail. We would fight. Things will work themselves out, Mary thought to herself.

"Get some rest, honey. We have much to do and talk about tomorrow." Thomas stood up and kissed her on the cheek.

Mary left the room. Huck had thanked the Donahues for their hospitality and left.

It was just Thomas and his parents. Nellie had taken the dishes inside to the kitchen.

"We're so proud of you, son. She seems like a beautiful soul." Frank patted his son on the shoulder.

"I always knew you would find someone." Marge hugged her son.

"I'm glad you guys like her." Thomas smiled. He stood near the doorway of the dining room.

"We love her. Just promise us one thing."

Marge looked into her son's timid eyes.

"Yes, mom?"

Frank cleared his throat. "Your mother and I have raised you to be submissive, peaceable, law abiding. When it comes to the name of love, we expect you to put up a good fight. There is no one else in the world that completes you like Mary does. Do not miss out on this opportunity." Frank smiled and gave his son a hug.

"You've found a girl worth fighting for." Marge looked her son in the eyes and added, "We're so proud of you. It will be an honor to have her as our daughter-in-law."

Thomas was stunned at his folk's reaction. He had expected them to look down at her. He had expected them to question his choice of a potential marriage mate. He never expected the waters to be so smooth. Maybe, just maybe things would work out after all, Thomas thought to himself as he left the dining room and headed upstairs for the night. This visit was surely not in vain.

FIFTEEN

"How do you like your eggs?" Nellie asked Mary. It was 8 a.m. and the sun had just come up over the horizon. Nellie opened the blinds to reveal a breathtaking view of Noblesville. The house was nestled on a hill that overlooked the small town.

Frank had left for the day and Marge was seated at the table across from Mary.

"Scrambled is fine." Mary wasn't used to being served so graciously.

"That's funny, that's how Tom likes his." Marge laughed taking a sip of her tea. "You guys have one more thing in common."

"Do you think we would ... never mind." Mary felt foolish, they had just met her not even 24 hours ago. How could his Mom know if the two of them were marriage quality material?

Marge caught on. "Oh, absolutely! You guys are perfect for each other. We moms know a good woman when we see one. It's something you'll learn one day when you have a child of your own." Marge knew one day the ideal woman would show up in her son's life. She just never thought he would have to travel to New York to find true love.

Nellie came in with a large plate of scrambled eggs, home fries and rye toast with strawberry jam lightly spread on it.

"I hope you like this jam. It came from the farm," Nellie said, looking at Mary's reaction.

Mary ate some and nodded her head in approval. "It's very good."

"I'm glad you like it." Nellie disappeared off into the kitchen.

Marge gave an awkward cough. Her tone switched from friendly to serious. "Tom told me what a wonderful meal he had at your friend Anna's. He said the food was delicious." She paused and collected her thoughts. "We're your parents there?"

Mary's expression revealed that she wanted no part of this discussion.

She frantically stood up and nearly hit her knee on the table.

"I really don't want to talk about it."

Nellie came in the kitchen, unaware of what just took place. "Thomas just pulled in. He's waiting for you," Nellie announced.

"Thank you. Breakfast was amazing! I must be on my way."

Nellie smiled. "Glad you enjoyed it. I have to get back to cleaning." She left the kitchen and went her way.

Marge felt bad. "Sweetheart, I apologize. I wasn't thinking." She reached out and gave her a hug

"It's okay. I really must go. Your son planned a full day today." Mary spoke quickly.

Marge gave her a warm smile. "See you tonight."

"Thanks again! Breakfast was delicious." Mary spoke with an uneasiness.

"It's our pleasure." Marge replied, while finishing the last of her meal.

Mary excused herself and walked out the kitchen and put her shoes on and headed out the door.

Nellie came out to find Marge with her head down in remorse.

"Oh, dear. I think I've upset her."

"It wasn't the best time to bring it up. It needs to be addressed. You know my youngest brother, Lucas, married a young colored woman from the West Indies. My father was dead set against it. They both persevered and ended up happily married."

"Maybe ... just maybe all will work out." Marge said hopefully. She was getting older and wanted to see her last son married off before death made his appointment with her.

"They are both intelligent adults. If it's meant to be, then it's meant to be. Would you like a refill on your tea? I just made a fresh pot."

Marge nodded and handed Nellie her cup. "I'm not far off from 70. Frank's diabetes is really taking a toll on his health. We aren't going to be around much longer."

"Marge, leave it in God's hands. If she's the one, then we have a grand wedding to look forward to. If not, I'm sure he will find someone. You're jumping the gun. Finish your tea. You have pinochle with the ladies at 11 a.m. Best you go on and get ready. I'll clean up and tidy."

Nellie always had plenty of horse sense. She was more like a close friend than a maid.

"You know, you would have made an excellent therapist." Marge chuckled.

"I've been around the block. Now you go on and have fun. I've got some cleaning to do."

Marge shook her head. "I just don't understand why her parents are so against it. Do you know why?"

Nellie took a seat next to Marge.

"Do you really wanna know my opinion?" Nellie asked.

Marge nodded. "You have always known the solution to whatever problems Frank and I have had to deal with over the years." You're more than just a maid, you are a real friend. I value your opinion." She took a sip of her tea.

Nellie chose her words carefully. "People who don't have money feel uneasy around those that do. Particularly immigrants."

Marge shook her head in disagreement.

"Nellie, Frank and I are nobody's. Frank has had a successful career. We aren't like most people. We are humans just like her family. That's a ridiculous reason to not allow your daughter to court someone of a higher class."

"Unfortunately, prejudice comes in different forms. It's just unfortunate that your family should feel the pain that comes with racism." Nellie shrugged her shoulders.

Marge was really hurt. As an empathetic person, she was sensitive to the feelings of others.

"It's not really racism. More like cultural differences."

"Racism, cultural differences. It's all the same in my book. I wouldn't let this bother you," Nellie gently replied while standing up and pushing her chair in.

Marge grimaced. "To tell you the truth it does bother me."

"Well, it shouldn't."

Nellie closed the door and scurried away.

It shouldn't bother me, but it does. It does bother me. They are so perfect for each other. If things don't work out. Tom will never be the same. It must work out. Marge thought to herself as she left the house and headed for town.

SIXTEEN

Modern Day

Mary smiled at the memories of the Donahue family. "I still remember the dinner we had that night. I remember the warmth and love that I was shown. The whole trip was quite something."

"You know, I have never heard of the Crosby mansion or the horse farm and I've lived on Long Island my whole life just about." Milagros had just been served a piece of Tiramisu.

The three of them were seated in the family room. Her cat, Chester, was seated on Tom's lap and was enjoying the company just as much as Mary was. "The mansion was torn down in the 70s. I wanna say '74. In the '80s, several homes were built on the property. You know the Walmart in the upper end of town? The Super Walmart? That's where the horse farm was. She died in '55. They had no relatives, so the town purchased the property. Such a shame." Mary shook her head in disbelief. It's a whole new world than it was almost 70 years ago."

"What about the letters?" Milagros asked in genuine anticipation.

"We communicated back and forth through letters." Mary stated, unsure of what she meant.

"I meant the good ones. These are amazing. One of them talks about you two going to Russia to study communism." Milagros shuffled through the letters.

Thomas was sitting with his feet propped up on the ottoman.

"After her visit, the letters intensified. This is truly remarkable," Tom mumbled to himself.

"One more question. Are you still for communism? I mean, after all you've seen over the ages. The Cold War, the Space Race, the fall of the Berlin Wall, 9-11," Milagros asked, enjoying cherishing every moment of the night.

"I always wondered myself," Mary softly added, crossing her leg.

"In my 94 years of life, I have concluded that man truly does not have the answer. I do think it's rather remarkable that I lived to see a black man as President. That shows the forwardness of America. I think President Obama is doing a fine job. I'm starting to get a sore throat from all my talking. I think Mary has some more to tell."

Tom gently pet the cat who was sound asleep.

"I think I'm a better storyteller ..." Mary giggled.

"No doubt about it." Thomas smiled softly.

The two of them laughed. It was cute to see two elderly adults enjoying each other's company Milagros thought. They must have been fun to be around in their younger years.

"There is a great deal more to tell. Love will have you do some peculiar things. I took a train all the way to Indiana. Back then you didn't dare travel alone if you were a young woman. If your parents said no, you listened. I did the opposite. I remember the night before I left, I stopped home to pick up some more clothes and personal belongings. My mother screamed at me in Italian. "Mary! Mary! Why you disrespect the family! You are trouble!"

Tom and Milagros sat in full attention.

"She threw pots and pans. Screaming curse words in Albanian and Italian. My father stood in the doorway crying. He kept saying 'why you cause us pain.'"

And my sister kept screaming, "You can't cook! What kind of a wife would you make! How dare you do this to our mom and dad after all they've done for you!"

Mary had a distant gaze in her eyes. "I don't regret any of it. As a matter of fact, Anna drove me to the train station that night. I remember her telling me everything was going to be okay. That I shouldn't feel like a bad person for causing such commotion. She reassured me that it was their fault for not understanding. Mind you, I wasn't engaged yet. Coming back home was a nightmare I'll never forget."

Mary continued, "That night, as I waited in Union Station in New Haven, I felt so small, so helpless. I found a man who loved me, who knew how to handle my idiosyncrasies. My own parents treated me like I committed a horrible, unforgivable atrocity, that somehow, even God could not forgive. Loving someone who was blonde haired, blue eyes, was a sin in their mind. I sure did pay."

Milagros gently interrupted. "I wanna hear the whole story."

"Young lady. You'll hear my story. I wish you wouldn't interrupt." Mary stiffened up. She was normally a very private person.

"Sorry. I just find this so intriguing." Milagros apologized. She had just finished her last piece of tiramisu.

Mary softened up. "If you want to hear my story. You'll need more coffee and another slice of tiramisu. Please get me another slice. I feel that once you hit 90 you can eat whatever you please whenever you please."

The three of them laughed. Mary had always kept a slim figure throughout her life, though she had gained a few pounds in her 80s.

Milagros went to the kitchen and came out with a large piece of tiramisu and an extra cup of coffee

Tom was enjoying every minute of it. This was probably the last time he would ever see her again.

After taking a bite, Mary smiled and went on with a faraway look in her eyes … "As I recall …

SEVENTEEN

(MARY'S STORY)

Mary had always obeyed her parents. Out of the two girls, Philomena knew she could count on Mary. When it came to getting groceries from the corner mart, Mary was always chosen over Gina. Gina would spend the change, Mary would always give back the change. For the first time in her life, she was willfully disobeying her family.

The train station was full of people. Young men saying their final goodbyes. Immigrant families huddled together. If it wasn't for the fighting, war time was truly a time of comradery. She sat on the hard wooden bench feeling so lost, so helpless.

"Miss." The middle aged ticket counter man called out interrupting her anxious thoughts.

"Yes?" Mary asked, unsure of what was going on.

"You're taking the train to Fort Wayne, aren't you? You better get a move on it. The train is about to leave. The next one ain't coming till 7:30 a.m."

"The next one isn't coming till 7:30 a.m. Ain't isn't a word." Mary corrected.

"Whatever lady. I just don't want you to miss the train." He rolled his eyes.

"Thank you." She smiled, then promptly boarded the train.

As she stepped on and walked clumsily through, people glanced at her. Her clothes were wrinkly. Her hair wasn't just so. She had been through an emotional hurricane the night before. The yelling and constant berating tore at her mind. One could compare it to a mosquito on a hot summer day. A relentless mosquito that just wouldn't quit.

Suddenly, she heard a loud boisterous cry of pain. An older woman was bawling her eyes out after reading a telegram about her son's death. The porter tried to give her comfort. Mary felt the same. No she did not lose a child to the ugliness of war. She just felt disowned from her own family. She wanted so badly to cry her frustrations out. She had to be strong although being strong wasn't easy. In fact it was nearly impossible. In her mind, trying to stay emotionally sound was an obstacle unlike no other.

Her father and mother wanted her to avoid Tom like he had the bubonic plague. Her sister made her feel insecure. What kind of a wife would you make? Those words echoed in her head. Her heart felt different. Her heart saw a reason to disobey. Her heart told her she would make a fine Mrs. Donahue. Facing the seemingly bleak reality ahead of her, she couldn't believe herself. Was this a dream?

What was a girl like her doing on a train headed to Timbuktu? She wondered what the people were like in Indiana. Would they accept her? Were his parents just like hers? Would they look at her as a poor little immigrant? Or would they see her as she truly was? A young woman determined to make it in a world that is set against bringing you down. Would they view her as a complement to their son? Or as a burden to their son? Would she fit their idea of what a proper wife should be? Her mind was racing and racing. Thoughts of doubt stayed in her mind. Mary would soon find out. She rested in her cramped cabin room and slept the jerky, uncertain ride away.

Four days later

Mary waited patiently under the drop-off port of the bustling train station. The sky was dark, and rain accompanied it. There was a young bearded man picking up his parents. An elderly farmer embraced his daughter as she entered his car. A middle-aged, horse-faced woman wearing a long, old-fashioned dress kissed her husband goodbye. All these people had a purpose. Was it a mistake? Mary felt a strong sense of regret. Suppose it didn't work with his parents. Then suppose it did. Her mind was stuck playing a game of tennis. The issue regarding Tom and the relationship was the ball. Her mind was in a deep, dark quandary. The only person to pull her out was Thomas. He was her hero.

An old 32 Ford pickup truck pulled up under the awning. The truck parked and Thomas came out of the passenger seat. A chubby guy with dirty blonde hair and overalls was the driver. He gave her a friendly wave. Mary glowed with delight.

Thomas wrapped his arms around Mary and gave her an amorous kiss. "So good to see you. It's been six weeks since we've last seen each other." He gave her a gentle kiss on the forehead. Mary blushed three shades of pink.

Taking her luggage and putting it in the back of the truck under a canopy, Thomas said in an excited tone, "How was your journey? You must be starved. My folks have dinner prepared for us at home."

"It was the longest train ride I've ever taken. It was a quiet ride though, so I read some and slept mostly. I can't wait to meet your parents," she said climbing in the middle of the truck.

His friend clumsily introduced himself. "Hi, my name is Huck. It's a real pleasure to meet you." He gave her a warm, neighborly smile.

"Nice to meet you." Mary smiled back.

"We are gonna get to know each other more tonight. My mom has a feast for us when we get home. I sure hope you brought your appetite," Thomas said, stepping in the truck.

"I haven't eaten much since I stepped foot in Union Station."

"I promise you. You won't be disappointed. Some good old hearty food is awaiting us." Thomas smiled caressing her hair. "Gosh, you look beautiful." His eyes studied her. She was exhausted and a tad bit unkempt. She had been through the battlefield of hell. He knew how they felt about him. He also knew they knew he would fight to the ends of the earth just to be with her.

The last thing she expected was to ride the remaining forty-five minutes in a pickup truck with two guys. Her body ached. Her mind was uneasy. As strange as it seemed, Mary felt like she was with totally normal people. The flashy lifestyles that New York City and Connecticut catered to wasn't Mary. She was attracted more to the rustic atmosphere of Indiana then her own home town.

She smiled a rather confident smile then laid her head on his shoulder and slept away the rest of the ride.

They reached the house at 6 p.m. By then the rain had settled down. Huck had driven past the nice parts and the not so nice parts of town. The people all had a tired worn look on their face but they had kind eyes and neighborly expressions.

Pulling into the driveway of the house, Mary couldn't help but notice the rather intimidating appearance of the house. It stood out among the rest of the farmhouses and shanties that inhabited Noblesville. The house was perched on top of a large, secluded hill.

Slowly walking up to the large heavy wood door with the brass door knocker, Mary felt a strong sense of fear. Maybe this wasn't a good idea. Thomas was holding her arm and Huck was behind them carrying the luggage.

Thomas opened the door to reveal a bubbly, short, overweight woman with curly reddish hair, animated eyes and a welcoming smile. She wore wire rimmed glasses that complimented her oval-shaped face.

"Welcome to the family!" She leaned forward and gave Mary a bear hug. "I'm Marge, Tom's mom."

"It's so nice to meet you. I've heard so much about you." Mary shook her hand.

An elderly man with white hair, thick glasses and a relaxed face stepped out of the living room. He was ecstatic to see her.

"Hi. My name is Frank. I'm Tom's dad. It's such a pleasure to have you come down for a visit. I really hope you enjoy your stay. Please let my wife show you to your room. That way you can get settled and relax. Dinner is almost done."

"It's a pleasure to meet you, sir."

She shook his hand. She had expected to have a whole different impression. These people seemed so real, so down to earth. So normal.

"Nope. No calling me sir. It's Frank and Marge. And the maid is Nellie. We want you to feel welcome. In my house, you're considered family."

"Thanks." Mary was really impressed at how nice they were.

"Follow me up the staircase." Marge volunteered as she led the way up the staircase. The house was large but homey. There were two flights of stairs. Mary followed Marge to the third bedroom on the left.

Marge opened the door and inside was a large, old-fashioned canopy bed with six fluffy pillows that were a welcoming sign.

"It's beautiful. The whole house is so … charming."

Marge laughed. "You haven't seen the whole house honey. But thank you we like it. I figured you were a girl who loves her pillows. I made sure Nellie brought up extra. You see that door across from the desk? That's your own private bathroom. Just give the tub some time to get hot. This house was built in 1834, so the plumbing is old and slow. Figured I would warn you."

Mary was in awe at how hospitable she was. He seemed so nice too. They would make the perfect in-laws. This all seemed so wonderful.

"Thank you. You guys really didn't have to do this. It's so unexpected."

"Oh, don't worry about it. We love having our son and his beautiful lady friend over. I almost forgot, the library is downstairs, if you ever wanna relax and unwind with a good book."

"Thanks."

"No problem, Hun. I'll see you in a few." She winked and closed the door. Huck had left the luggage by the door, so she started unpacking her clothes. This was going to be the best and the worst time of her life.

EIGHTEEN

"Wow, this is a real banquet." The five of them were seated in the dining room. Nellie, the short haired, elderly maid refilled Mary's glass of water. "It's so nice to have you here. I hope you like my food." She laughed and went back to the kitchen.

The table was adorned with roasted chicken, homemade corn bread, freshly shucked corn, mashed potatoes, collard greens, salad, and meatloaf.

"Everything is so wonderful." Mary blushed.

She kept her eye on Thomas, he seemed so relaxed, so handsome. Things were looking good.

"Good, glad you like it." Marge quipped.

Taking a bite of his chicken, swallowing it down with a glass of lemon water, Frank asked.

"So, tell me all about yourself. All I know is that from what Tom tells us, you're smart and from what we see, very stunning. So, the table is all yours."

"My name is Mary Mascia. I'm from New Haven, Connecticut. Are you familiar with it?"

"No. Not at all tell us." All three of them gave Mary their keen attention. "Please tell us about it."

"It's a large city. My family moved there from Italy after I was born in January of '20. They moved in 21, is what I meant. I was born in Italy, but I have no recollection of it. My family came from a mountain village."

"Wow, that's fascinating. We went as a family to Italy back in the latter '20s. Marge and I wanted to take the boys for a once in a lifetime trip. I absolutely loved everything about it, the cuisine, the people, the history. Just a remarkable experience."

Frank sat back in his chair and smiled at the memory. "I remember taking the boys to see the Leaning Tower of Pisa. Young Tom stared at the structure and tugged at his mother's dress and suggested that we all, in unison, push against the tower to make it upright again. Kids say the darndest things."

The whole table cracked up in laughter.

"Dad." Thomas sat low in his chair, totally embarrassed.

Mary didn't care. She thought it was cute.

"You were 10 or 12. I can't remember. I do remember that from that day on, I knew you would be something in life."

"So, how did you two meet?" Marge asked, chewing on her corn as Nellie came in and refilled the plate.

"We met at the Crosby Mansion. I was having some … anxiety that night and…"

"Sure, that place is huge. Anyone would have anxiety going there. I'm sorry you were saying..." Marge interrupted.

A LETTER FROM *Thomas*

Mary was glad they understood. Not everyone understands anxiety. Thomas inherited his folk's kindness.

"We met at the fountain and we just started talking. And the rest is history." She looked at Thomas and he looked at her. Their eyes were locked in the chain of love.

"Oh, that sounds so romantic. I love it!" Marge clapped her hands together.

"What are you majoring in?" Huck asked, on his third piece of cornbread.

"I plan to be an English teacher."

"That's a great job!" Marge exclaimed enthusiastically.

Frank nodded in agreement.

"So tell us. What made you pursue that career? You're obviously a very smart, well- spoken young woman. You could have chosen anything and aced it. Why an English teacher? Like my wife said, it's a great job. I'm just curious."

Mary's eyes lit up. "I've always loved the English language and I love kids. That seemed to be the ideal candidate for me."

"I admire a young lady like yourself. Instead of staying home and being a homemaker, you're pursuing your dreams." Marge said, sipping her water while gesturing for Nellie to bring out fresh lemons.

"I could never be a homemaker. Who wants to clean and cook all day long?" Mary waited for a reaction.

"Not me. Frank was a surgeon and I was a secretary for a firm in Noblesville," said Marge, relating to her. "Frank didn't need me to work. I insisted and worked till I was 60. I'm 66 and Frank is 70. I love people and people love me. I wouldn't do well staying home cooking and cleaning. That's why we have Nellie."

"Watch it," Nellie joked. She had the appearance of a kind, old grandmotherly type.

"We've had dear old Nellie since 1919. She really is the best. Her husband died suddenly, and she needed a job and a place to stay. So, we hired her. Best decision we've ever made."

The elderly maid smiled. The Donahue family had cared for her quite well over the years.

"The Lord couldn't have blessed me enough." Nellie said with every ounce of truth. "The kindest people in the world are right here in front of you. I really do mean that." She spoke directly to Mary.

Marge blushed. "Oh, Nellie! That was so nice of you to say."

The elderly maid shook her head in firm resolute. "Who else would take care of an old geezer like myself?"

Frank laughed. "You aren't old. You're an antique. One that we're quite blessed to have."

Nellie smiled and proceeded to the kitchen.

Mary was in the company of hospitable people. The fear she had of not fitting in with the family disappeared. Tomorrow, Thomas had planned to take her to the apple orchard then to a gathering at Huck's house. Although not one to enjoy social outings, Mary was looking forward to it.

"What a great story—how very kind of you all for taking her in like that. And thank you for showing me such wonderful hospitality." The grandfather clock read a quarter past ten. It was a long day for her, though it flew by fast.

"I don't want to be rude but it's getting late and I must retire for the night."

Mary stood up and pushed her chair in.

"You've had a long day dear, go ahead and rest up. See you in the morning. Sweet dreams," Thomas said getting up to take her plate.

"Goodnight guys. See you in the a.m." Mary smiled and went off her way. Tomorrow would be another day.

NINETEEN

This young woman seems so distant, Nellie thought to herself as she opened the door to the kitchen.

Mary sat across the kitchen table from Marge.

"How do you like your eggs?" Nellie asked Mary. It was 8 a.m. and the sun had just come over the horizon. Nellie opened the blinds to reveal a breathtaking view of Noblesville. The house was on a hill that overlooked the town.

Frank had already left for the day and Marge was seated at the table admiring her daughter-in-law to be. She knew Tom and Mary were the ideal match for each other.

"Scrambled is fine." Mary wasn't used to being served so graciously.

"That's funny, that's how Tom likes his." Marge laughed taking a sip of her tea. "You guys have one more thing in common."

Mary forced a smile. She had her head down in deep thought.

"Are you okay? Did you sleep well last night?" Marge asked with concern.

"I slept just fine. It's just that ... Oh, never mind." She let out a heavy sigh.

"What's wrong?" Marge asked.

"Do you think we have a chance?" Mary felt foolish, they had just met her not even 24 hours ago. How could his mom know if the two of them were marriage quality material?

Marge caught on. "Oh, absolutely! You guys are perfect for each other. Us moms know a good woman when we see one. It's something you'll learn one day when you have a child of your own." Marge knew one day the ideal woman would show up in her son's life. She just never thought he would have to travel to New York to find true love.

Nellie came in with a large plate of scrambled eggs, home fries and rye toast with strawberry jam lightly spread on it.

"I hope you like this jam. It came from the farm." Nellie said looking at Mary's reaction.

Mary ate some and nodded her head in approval.

"It's very good."

"I'm glad you like it. Don't be shy about taking seconds."

Mary smiled. "I'll be sure to. It almost reminds me of back home. My Pop keeps a small chicken coop in the back of our yard. These eggs taste so fresh."

"Enjoy, honey."

Nellie smiled, then disappeared off into the kitchen. Marge gave an awkward cough. Her tone switched from friendly to serious.

"Tom told me what a wonderful meal he had at your friend Anna's. Something that concerns me is your parents. I don't mean to get personal. It just doesn't seem right that parents of a different background should be so dead set against two young people with ambition. Just because my son was born on another part of the globe."

Mary was defensive. "I would rather not talk about it just now."

"I apologize. It's just that my son really adores you. It troubles me that ethnicity would even be an issue. I realize it's too early in the morning to discuss controversial issues but at the same time I feel it should be discussed."

"We can have this conversation later. I see your son just pulled up in the driveway. I'll see you later tonight."

Mary excused herself, walked out the kitchen, put her shoes on and headed out the door.

Nellie came out to find Marge with her head down in remorse.

"You didn't bring up what happened with her folks?" Nellie asked.

Marge nodded. "It needs to be addressed."

"Not at 9 a.m. in the morning." Nellie replied, while letting out a sigh. "Those two are perfect for each other. Thomas seems so happy. No need to fret about it. Time will give you a chance to talk about it."

"Doctor Gillespie was over yesterday morning. Frank's not doing too well. It's just a matter of time." Marge paused, as tears of sadness trickled down her face. "All we want is to see Thomas married off and happy."

"He will be married off soon to Mary. Don't think about the worst that may or may not come."

Nellie gave Marge a comforting hug.

"I just can't believe our son was treated so badly." Marge wiped a tear from her eyes, "They are so perfect for each other."

"Everything will be okay. Now you must get going. The girls are waiting for you." Nellie stood up and walked away.

Nellie always had the right thing to say. Perhaps all will be well. Marge thought to herself.

TWENTY

"This place is so lovely," Mary noted as Tom pulled into the Baden Orchard. Young mothers were picking apples with their kids. The air was crisp, and the weather was ideal. Tom brought along a leather backpack. The old man had passed on the previous month. so the Baden boys were in the middle of fixing up the general store. Mary didn't seem to notice. They walked down to the orchard where she was surrounded by hundreds of apple trees.

"Have you ever gone apple picking?" Thomas asked, his eyes full of excitement.

"Never been. I've also never traveled on a train, left the East Coast, or fallen in love." Her eyes lit up.

Thomas laughed a whimsical laugh. "It's easy. You reach up and pick an apple; if it's good you put it in the basket. If it's bad..." he picked a rotten apple. "you just toss it on the ground." As if on cue, a fat squirrel came and carried it away.

They both laughed.

"Come on, go ahead and pick one." Mary was just barely 5 feet tall. Thomas, on the other hand, had a towering presence of 6'2". So Thomas gently lowered the branch for her. Mary took an apple and decided to try it out.

"You're supposed to eat it later, silly."

"I couldn't resist. It tastes so fresh." Mary was full of enthusiasm. She was happy. As long as she had Tom in her life, she was happy. Happiness had come in her life disguised as an Englishman from a middle America town. She hoped happiness wasn't a passerby in her life though she knew this relationship would soon be over the moment she returned home. "I know, these are amazing."

"Thomas, I have a question," Mary asked, not wanting to ask the question that has been on her mind all morning.

After picking up a juicy apple that had fallen to the ground, he answered, noticing her whole mood changed. "Yes. What's wrong?"

"The day you came over to see my family. What did my father say to you? Be honest. You were gone a long time."

"It doesn't matter. That's in the past. I would rather not say. I love you. My family is keen on you. That's all that matters."

Mary pleaded. "I wanna know. For my own sake. I can handle it."

"Mary I just couldn't."

Mary looked him in the eyes. "I need to know. Please tell me."

"Well, alright. He said that I wasn't welcome in his family. He said that your mother ..."

"Wants to go to my wedding and be proud of the man I'm marrying." Mary finished his sentence verbatim.

"Yes. How did you know?"

"My whole life. My mother has always said that to me. Oh, Thomas, what are we going to do? I just couldn't live with that kind of hatred. You don't know my mother. She would make my life, our life a living hell."

"Mary, it doesn't matter. In the long run, it doesn't matter. Trust me on this."

"It does matter. I can't do this." Mary started to cry. Tom put his arm around her and hugged her.

"It's going to be okay. We're gonna get through this. They will have to learn to respect our differences. Think about it. Their oldest daughter married to a successful doctor. We will make money. Travel the world. Make memories that will last a lifetime."

Struggling through the tears, she stuttered, "They won't. They'll never understand. I don't know what to do. Oh, Thomas this was a mistake. What was I thinking?"

They had entered a secluded spot near the top of the hill. It was a favorite spot of Tom's.

He pulled off his backpack and unzipped it. Out came a folding camera.

Mary looked up. She sat down in the grass. Her mind was in a quandary. She truly loved this man. He loved her. His family was so kind, so human. Hers was so cold, so bitter against change. She was the change. Her relationship with Tom was the change that her mother feared so much.

"Come on. Smile. I know you can. You've got a lot to smile about." Tom encouraged.

"Oh, Tom. I wish I could smile." Mary spoke softly.

"You can. Think of something funny or something that you appreciate."

Mary thought about it, then gave in. "Well, okay." Mary gave the most beautiful smile a camera could capture. The flash caught it.

"What made you smile? That was such a gorgeous smile."

Mary looked into Tom's eyes. "Remember that night we met. You said you thought I was a princess because of the dress I wore. I just thought that was the most beautiful thing a guy could say."

"Well, you are a princess. I'm your knight in shining armor. Let's say we head on over to the general store and take these apples home. Huck is having a social event at his farm house tonight. It wouldn't be right if you didn't come."

"I would love that." Mary blushed.

The Bradbury farmhouse was a stable in the town of Noblesville. The family had been in the town as farmers for generations upon generations. Walter and Eunice Bradbury supplied the grocers with fresh corn every summer. They also had a large 8-acre maze that the townsfolk loved to explore every year. For 25 cents a person, families from all over the state would bring their kids and get lost in the maze. Nights like these, when the maze was shut down, the family of seven had large events.

The farm house was situated on 250 acres of land. It was painted red with white shutters and a giant willow tree guarded the front. They arrived just before 5:30 p.m. Young men in overalls and straw hats brought their wives and girlfriends for a night of fun.

Eunice Bradbury was a kind and gracious woman who wore her blonde hair in a bun. Eunice knew everyone and everyone knew Eunice. Walter was known for his homemade apple pies and good sense of humor. He was tall, well built, with gray hair. He always wore overalls and plaid shirts, unless it was Sunday. He was the local preacher. A talented man of God. He was well known for his inspirational sermons.

"Well ... Who is this beauty?" Eunice asked as Tom and Mary stepped out of the car. Walter had followed his wife to the car to greet them.

"This is my beautiful girlfriend, Mary. Mary, this is Eunice. And her husband, Walter."

Eunice gave her a warm embracing hug. "Welcome to our home. I've heard all about you. Gosh, it's so nice to finally meet you."

"How do you do? I'm Walter, her husband." He extended his hand and gave her a friendly shake.

"Nice to meet you both. It's such an honor to be here."

Walter grinned. "A friend of Tom's is a friend of ours. Don't be shy now. We got some good food cooking. I hope you like to dance cause we're gonna have some good dancing music later."

He gave her a friendly tap on the shoulder and went on his way.

Eunice took her and Tom to the backyard where a large tent had been set up which covered nine tables of food. "Let me introduce you to some of the people before you eat. This is Roy and Henrietta Bishop."

The couple smiled and shook her hand. "How do you do, young lady?"

"I'm fine, thank you." Henrietta gave Mary a genuine smile and moved on.

Eunice next introduced her to a young couple enjoying their smoked ribs. "Here is Ober and Flora Winslow."

"How do you do? What's your name?" Flora asked.

"Mary Mascia. I'm visiting Thomas Donahue and his family for three weeks."

Flora wore her brunette hair in a pony tail that cascaded down to her waist. "Well, it's a pleasure to meet you. Where are you from?"

"New Haven." Mary answered softly.

"Oh, wow. You made quite the trip. Did you fly or take the train?" Ober asked, cleaning his glasses.

"I would never go on a plane. I took the train; it was a four-day ordeal."

"We sure are happy to have you." Flora gave Mary a warm smile.

"I'm so happy to be here! The people here are so nice and friendly. You all seem like distant family." Almost everyone had a smile on their face. People rarely smile on the East Coast, Mary thought to herself.

Flora smiled. "I'm from North Carolina, so I'm used to it. You're right though, people are nice down here. You better get some of those ribs before they're gone." She and Ober waved goodbye.

"Hey guys!" Huck called out, he was making his way through the crowd. An attractive female was with him.

"You guys always throw the nicest of parties." Thomas complimented. He had a plate full of food.

"Oh, it's our pleasure. Are you enjoying your stay?" He asked Mary.

"Very much. People are so friendly."

"I'm glad you're having a good time. This is Ruth." The young, red-headed woman reached out and shook Mary's hand.

"Nice to meet you. So how did you guys meet?" She asked innocently.

"We met at a party. We started talking and here we are today. How about you?"

"Huck and I met through mutual friends. He's the sweetest guy in the world." Ruth blushed. "So, are you guys both going to Columbia?"

"He's at Yale and I'm striving to get my master's degree in education. He will be finishing up at Kansas State University. I just wanted to come down and meet his family." Mary smiled.

"I knew his major. What made you interested in teaching if you don't mind my asking?" Her eyes lit up in genuine interest.

"I just always appreciated the English language. Plus, I love kids. I'm gonna be teaching kindergarten to third grade."

"Well, that's impressive." Ruth nodded, sipping her drink.

"Hey, babe! I want you to meet a friend of mine." Huck came over and escorted Ruth. "Great to see you again, Mary. I hope you have a swell time."

"Everything is so wonderful!" Mary grinned.

Huck and Ruth both smiled.

"Good luck! I'll see you around."

Ruth left and an older couple came up to Mary. The wife was plain and wore her hair in a bun. The husband was tall and lean. He wore a straw hat and was smoking a cigarette.

"My name is Jean, and this is my husband, Howard. We've heard all about you. I play pinochle with Marge on Wednesdays. It's nice to meet you." The elderly couple extended their hands.

"Wow, word gets out!" Mary said, surprised.

"It's a small, close-knit town. Everybody knows everybody. I've known Tom since he was knee high to a grasshopper. He's a wonderful young man and from what I've heard, you're a wonderful young lady. I wish you guys the best. See you at your wedding."

Mary awkwardly smiled. "Oh. We aren't engaged just yet."

"Oh, sweetheart! You don't just come all the way from Connecticut and not go back unengaged. I'm sure he will propose soon." Jean smiled.

She winked and moved on.

There was something about these people. They seemed so friendly, so hopeful, so willing to accept her in their circle.

Never did she imagine that the Midwestern way of life would be more accepting then her own family. She felt like a foreigner in her own family. Woman don't work, they cook. They don't marry someone of a different background. They marry one of their own. They wouldn't dare travel halfway across the country to spend time with the one they love. Women just don't do that. Mary wasn't a typical woman. She took pride in that. It made her happy to know that his family embraced her. They treated her like she was their own daughter. Yes, this could work. There was a possibility that after all this love could blossom into a happy marriage. She would be Mrs. Donahue and he would be her respected husband, Dr. Donahue. They would live a life full of comfort. She would not struggle like her mother did nor would she be treated poorly like her father was. In her mind, this could work out very well. Then it couldn't. Her mother would excommunicate her from the family. Her father would shake his head in disgust at her disobedience. Gina would rub in her mother's face that she was the good daughter who listened, obeyed and followed tradition. Why? Why did tradition have to rule her life? Was tradition more important to her family then her own happiness?

Suddenly, her thoughts were interrupted. "Let's dance." Thomas took her hand and led her to the wooden dance floor. The full moon illuminated the dance floor.

Mary stepped back. "Are you crazy? I can't dance." She laughed awkwardly.

Thomas laughed. "It's easy. Just move to the rhythm. Don't be so bashful."

Mary complied and joined Tom on the dance floor. Other young couples acknowledged her and smiled.

They were playing the banjo. Everyone was dancing and having a good old time. Mary hated dancing but enjoyed this dance. She looked intensely into the eyes of her boyfriend. He looked back, giving her the 'this is going to be all right' look.

"I love you so much." Thomas bent down and kissed her on the lips. That moment of time seemed to slow down. Everything else. Everyone else. Did not matter. She was lost in the world of Mary and Tom. Nothing else mattered.

TWENTY-ONE

"How did you two kids enjoy the outing?" Nellie asked greeting them at the door. "Your folks are at the picture house. Won't be back 'til late."

Mary's eyes illuminated in happiness.

"It was lovely. He took me to the Baden Farm, and we picked apples. Such a beautiful place. Then, we went to this large event at Huck's house. I had such a splendid evening. Tom even got me out on the dance floor which is something I would have never done. Not normally any way. It was the perfect end to a perfect night."

"I'm glad you guys had a ball. I have to finish up the stuffed cabbage I made for your folks." Nellie went back in the kitchen.

Mary turned to Tom. "Can I speak to you … alone?"

"Sure, let's go into the library. We can have a moment to speak." Thomas led her down to the hall and to the right. She then stepped in the library and sat on the couch. Tom closed the door behind him and sat on the chair.

"Is everything okay?"

Mary sighed. "Do you think ... do you think that we have a chance? Or is this all futile? Is my coming here just a big joke?"

"No. Not at all. Why would you say that?" Thomas looked at her with concern, while rubbing her back.

"I never told you. When I left for the train station. The emotional abuse that my family gave me ... was just too much. My mother was throwing stuff at me while screaming at the top of her lungs. My dad was crying, saying things like, why would you do this to us?"

She continued, "Like it's a crime to love someone who isn't of your culture. In their minds, I'm a criminal. I just can't take it anymore. Your family is so sweet and kind and understanding. And mine is so ..." She broke out in tears.

"Mary. It's okay. It's going to be alright. I'll be a doctor soon and you'll be a teacher. They must understand. They just have to." His voice trailed off.

"They won't! They refuse to see that you're the only man that makes me happy. I feel so alive when I'm around you. I feel like I can overcome anything with you."

"Well then, you can overcome this. This is the 1940s, things have changed. Time has moved on. People need to know that it's perfectly normal to love someone who is different from you. It's okay to go against them. If our relationship is going to make you a happy and better person then what right do, they have to come in here and tear apart something that was meant to be?"

"They're my parents! You don't understand. The control that Italian mothers have over their daughters. They can make you or break you. Especially my mother."

"Do I make you happy?"

"What?" Mary asked confused.

"Just answer the question. Does being in my presence make you feel good about yourself?"

"Of course. I feel like a new woman around you."

"Will you be all set financially and emotionally with me as your future husband? If it should happen."

"With our incomes, we won't be millionaires, we won't be paupers. We will be comfortable in life."

"Do you think that I would make a good son-in-law to your folks? Should we have kids, do you think that I would make a decent father? A good role model for our son or daughter to look up to?"

"Yes, and Yes. Why are you asking me all these questions?"

"That's all that matters. If you convey that to them. Everything will be okay. That's a parent's biggest worry when it comes to their children marrying another person. You have to trust that we could make this happen."

"I can't. Oh, Tom, I don't know what to do!" Mary took off crying hysterically. She ran past a much-confused Nellie and ran up the staircase to her room.

Laying on the soft bed with her head in a pillow sobbing, a soft knock could be heard at the door. Mary just wanted to be left alone. She felt foolish. Her relationship with her family was at stake. She was madly in love with Tom. His family took her in as their own.

There was a repeated soft knock on the door.

"Mary, dear. I would like to talk to you." Nellie spoke in a kind, concerned tone. "Please, can I come in?"

"S-sure." Mary stammered in tears.

Nellie walked in and sat on the edge of the bed. Her wrinkled hand reached out to Mary's.

"I wanted to tell you a little story that I think will give you hope."

Mary lowered the pillow and gave Nellie her full attention. "Go on. I'm listening."

"I grew up with a father who was a racist against the colored folk. His only son, my brother, fell in love with the sweetest, nicest young woman from the West Indies. It caused quite a stir as you can imagine. My brother truly loved this woman and she loved him. They weren't going to let anything, or anyone get in the way. So, one day, he proposed to her. My father heard about and confronted him. He used some colorful language. After a whole hour of him being berated, he told my Father loud and clear. I love you, you're my father. You worked hard your whole life taking care of three kids all by yourself. I may love you, but I love Liliana even more. She completes me. My father never spoke to him ever again. In the end, he married a beautiful soulmate. They just celebrated their 50th anniversary this past September. You must do what's best for you. Now that's my advice you can take it or leave it."

Nellie gave Mary a warm, resounding, comforting hug.

"Thank you. This whole thing has just been such a dilemma. I just feel so depressed. I love Tom. He's such a wonderful, kind-hearted soul. I also love my family. Italian's are a close-knit culture. I just could not bear to cause such a disturbance." Mary sighed.

Nellie looked at Mary and said, "I understand."

Mary looked doubtful. "You do?"

"Yes, I do. I'm 79 years old, honey. I've seen the good, the bad and the downright ugly sides of life."

"I'm sure you have." Mary agreed.

The elderly maid cleared her throat. She went over to open the windows. A fresh midnight breeze came through. "Mary, your parents are older. They won't be around forever. You and Tom are young. You guys have forever together. 25. 30. 50. And if you're lucky, 60 years together. You have a family to look forward to. You have a son or daughter to look forward to seeing them grow and get married. You guys have the whole world ahead of you. Regret is a terrible emotion. I can't tell you what to do. That's up to you, it's late now. I'll see you in the morning." She closed the door and went downstairs.

Mary thought about what she said. Maybe, just maybe, she was right. She had in her mind imagined a happy future with Tom in mind. They truly complemented each other. He was smart, well spoken, and had an excellent relationship with his parents. She was an intelligent, soft spoken, kind-hearted young woman. They were the ideal match. If her family truly loved her, they would accept her marriage to Tom. Nellie was right. They did have forever together...

The next morning

"It's just so damn frustrating." Thomas said, while waiting for a fish to bite. His father and Huck had arranged for Tom to spend some alone time with them. Marge had taken Mary for the day. Thomas needed some time alone to think about his future with Mary. His two best friends were with him. One of his favorite past times was fishing, so Huck took the day off to hang with his friend. Mary's battle with her parents really affected Tom. He wasn't sleeping. He was more secluded from everyone. He just wasn't himself. He needed to talk and for people to listen.

Tom continued. "I have everything planned out. I'm going to serve my country. I'm gonna finish my education in Kansas City and eventually become a doctor. She and I will be happily married. I'll be saving lives, she'll be teaching lives. People will admire us from afar and say man I wish I was as happy as they are."

The three of them were seated on the wooden bench in front of the lake that was near Huck's house. It was unlikely that they would catch anything. Tom didn't care. He needed to unwind.

Frank Donahue wasn't a fan of fishing. His son needed him, more now than ever. Marriage isn't something to mess around with. Truth be told, he and Marge loved Mary. She and Tom were two peas in a pod. A few times she would finish his sentences and vice versa. Marge was very much worried about her emotional state. It didn't seem normal for someone to have that much fear of her parent's approval. His wife had spent much of the evening talking about Mary, privately in their bedroom. Marge had wondered if there was some form of emotional abuse that she suffered from. Frank had reassured her that it was just a culture thing though deep down he wondered the same thing. How she was acting was far from normal.

"Your mother and I have no qualms with her. She's a lovely young lady. I do think that you should consider seriously her emotional state. Can you handle someone who is so fragile? She seems to be a very emotional young lady."

"Dad, please." Tom retorted. His gaze was set straight ahead. He felt a tug, then it went away.

"I'm being very honest with you. Emotional instability is hard to live with." He shook his head and spit on the ground. "Something isn't right. She seems so afraid of what her folks will say if you guys tie the knot."

"Dad, please!" Tom shouted. "She just has to get over it."

"Your father has a point. Do you really want to spend the rest of your life living with someone who is unstable?"

Huck asked, wheeling in his catch. He placed the fish in a bucket filled with ice.

"She is not unstable. She's insecure. That's alright. I can deal with someone feeling insecure."

Thomas sat with his gaze straight ahead. He had dated other women. No one was Mary. She had a certain allure about her that that captured his interest. Everyone has problems. That's a given. It's how you can deal with someone's problems that matter. Thomas thought to himself.

Frank smoked his pipe. He rarely smoked. This situation had caused a certain amount of stress on him and Marge. Thomas was in his later 20s and not married. Though they never verbally made an issue out of it, it was very much a concern to his wife.

"Okay, fine. Do you think you could handle her family's wrath against you?" Frank asked peering into his son's eyes. "Your brothers are both successfully married. They didn't just willie nilly themselves when it came to courtship. They took it seriously, counted their costs and made it work. I don't want any of my son's being the talk of the town and divorcing because of a faulty relationship with the in-laws."

Thomas rolled his eyes. "Dad, you don't understand."

Frank continued. "I understand a lot more than you do. You're still a young man. You don't know how serious this situation could turn out. Italian women can be extremely manipulative."

Thomas jumped up and kicked the bucket of ice. Huck gave him a look of shock. Frank stood up and grabbed his son.

"Hey, you sit down and act like a grown man. I'm trying to save your behind from making a mistake." Frank softened up. "Your mother and I approve of your marriage to Mary. We just don't want you two splitting up down the road because of this prejudice rubbish."

"That's right. It's not fair." Huck added, he placed his hand on Tom's shoulder like a good old friend. "You've always had my back in life. As kids we stood up for each other. As an adult, if I see you're headed down the wrong road, I'm gonna speak. I happen to like her. She's a nice woman. She's got problems. Who doesn't? If you can make it happen, then do it."

Huck gave him a friendly slap on the back.

"That's right. Huck and I are gonna tell it to you like a man. It's getting late. I say we head on back home." Frank said, standing up and straightening his bad back.

"Hold on, guys. How long is Mary up for? I take it you're gonna propose. It's been several months since you guys met." Huck asked taking the bucket to the trunk of his truck.

Tom sighed. "She leaves next Friday. I don't even know where to pick up a ring. Or how I would go about proposing?"

"Where did you take her that she really liked?" Frank asked.

"Baden's Farm she loved. I showed her my favorite spot, as kids we used to go the secluded part of the apple orchard. I took this really beautiful photo of her."

Frank gave a warm smile. "There you go."

Huck shook his head in agreement. Huck and Frank both watched as Thomas thought about the matter.

Huck chimed in. "And as far as a ring, there's Nesbit Jewelers on Main street next to Quinn Avenue. The little jewelry store owned by Mr. Nesbit. I'm sure he has something in your price range."

Frank smiled. "I tell you what. Tomorrow we will go, and I'll pay for half of it. I realize it's not the most conventional thing to do. You don't have money to spend. You have to save up for your studies, son."

Thomas gave his father a look of embarrassment. "Dad, I couldn't."

Frank raised his hand. "I insist. Now stop. You have a diamond ring to pick out for that beautiful young lady."

"Next Friday will be here before you know it. I suggest you go as soon as possible." Huck had started up the truck. The three of them hopped in and drove off. Although he didn't catch any fish, he caught some helpful insight.

"Dad, what about The Beaumont?"

Frank rolled down the window. "What about it? I haven't gone since the last time you came with me. Let's say tomorrow at 10 a.m. We will get there nice and early and you propose when you get the chance."

Frank had wanted this to work out. He was glad it did. She would make good use out of his last name. Mrs. Donahue, the English teacher. Mary Donahue, our beautiful daughter-in-law. His grandchildren would have a mother named Mary. And a father who was a doctor. Frank smiled at the thought. This would work out.

TWENTY-TWO

Earl Nesbit had run his family's store since 1895. He was 24 when he took over the store from his ailing father. In the 49 years that he ran it, Earl saw numerous young couples come in and leave happy. His place was the only place for miles and miles. Business had been slow, so when the two distinguished looking men walked through the door, he took note.

"How can I help you?" Earl asked, while cleaning up the register area.

"Hi, how are you? We're looking for a nice, big, beautiful diamond ring," Thomas replied checking out the variety. It was small shop with a limited variety.

"What's your price range? I have some over here. They're a tad expensive."

"300 to 500 dollars," Frank responded. The old jeweler's face revealed total shock. "Very well then, over here."

He escorted the two men to the back of the shop where a 14 karat white gold ring sat on display behind a glass encasement.

"That's beautiful. How much?" Thomas inquired, while nervously studying the quality. Would Mary like this? He thought to himself.

"She's a beauty. I have the price set at $245 dollars." Earl took the ring out of the case and let Thomas hold it.

"The quality is exceptional. I think she will love it. What do you think, Dad?"

Frank looked at the ring. "I say it's an exceptional ring for an exceptional woman."

Earl smiled and looked at Thomas. "You like?"

"It's a deal." Thomas said happily. He took out his bank envelope and purchased the ring.

"Is your girl from the area?" Earl asked, placing the ring in its proper package.

"She's leaving for Connecticut on Friday. I won't see her for a while. It's complicated," Thomas sighed.

"You fellows are the only ones I've seen all day. You can tell me the story unless you rather not." Earl sat in his chair behind the register. He was enjoying the company.

"Well, her parents are against our being together. It's a matter of cultural differences."

Earl propped his head up in interest. "Oh, I see she's a negro. Her folks don't like you cause your white."

"No. Not at all. Her folks are Italian immigrants. They don't approve of their daughter marrying a soon to be doctor." Thomas corrected. "They want her to marry a fellow Italian so she can stay home and make pasta while popping out babies. It's beyond ridiculous."

"That's the immigrant mentality for you. Old-world immigrants I suppose," Frank remarked shaking his head in disgust.

"Not to be disrespectful but you were once an immigrant. Not terribly long ago. It has nothing to do with being an immigrant. It's a culture thing. Something that quite frankly I don't understand at all," Thomas replied with his head down in sadness.

Frank put his hand on his son's shoulder. "Don't worry about it, son. You have everyone on your side."

Earl stood up from his chair and paced his store. "I've run this place since 1895. I've heard numerous love stories. Young happy couples coming in with dreams and ambitions. It always made me happy to help the men pick out which ring for his soon to be wife. Although I have heard some sad stories, I've never heard anything quite like that. You forget about that nonsense. If you love her, and she loves you, then that's all. Am I right, Pop?" Earl jokingly asked Frank, who had been quietly thinking to himself.

"Oh, absolutely. Trust me, we have had several long talks. My son seems to think she's the one. My wife and I wish him the best."

Earl smiled. "You have a beautiful woman to bring that to. I wish you all the joy and happiness this ugly world has got to offer."

"Thanks, sir. I suppose we will be on our way."

Earl waved them off. Thomas and his father resembled a young child walking gingerly with his dad on the first day of school as they walked down Main street together one last time as a father and a bachelor.

TWENTY-THREE

"I leave on Friday. Shouldn't I be packing my clothes?" Mary asked Thomas, feeling a tad anxious. She and Marge had spent the whole previous day together shopping at various department stores. For some strange reason, Thomas was unusually quiet that Tuesday night. Mary couldn't quite figure out what was going on. He nervously asked her to go with him back to the orchard. Mary wasn't keen on going back to the orchard, but a gut feeling told her to be quiet and gracious.

"No. You only had two bags with you. It's not like you have all these clothes to worry about. I promise this will be worth it, trust me." Thomas was focused on the road. It was a 25-minute drive to the orchard. Mary kept quiet and observed the scenery. A young couple in their 30s walked shoulder to shoulder, the young, long-haired blonde walked their bulldog who obediently walked in unison. Secretly, she had hoped Thomas would've proposed by now. Next time she came, he would she thought disappointingly to herself. If there was to be a next time.

Thomas pulled his car in the driveway of the orchard. It was late Wednesday afternoon on a warm, memorable day.

"I uh ...I don't want to pick any apples." Thomas said clumsily.

Mary laughed like an innocent child. "Well, what do you suppose we do here? You're acting weird. Is everything okay?"

"I just want to go to my spot and watch the sunset with you and talk. Why is that so strange to you? I haven't seen you for an entire day."

Mary shrugged her shoulders. "I'm just enjoying the moment with you." Her big brown eyes lit up. She lay her head against his shoulders.

"That makes two of us." Thomas said looking proudly at his girl.

"What are we doing up here? The sun doesn't set for at least another hour," Mary observed. They were both seated down on the green grass. The wind gently blowing in his golden blonde hair. They sat for a while. Neither one of them spoke.

"Mary."

"Yes," Mary said, her eyes almost asleep. She lay next to him. They were both looking up at the October sky. It had a pinkish color to it.

"I've been meaning to tell you something that's been on my mind. I love you." He said carefully choosing his words.

"Oh, Tom, I love you too!" Mary cheerfully replied.

"I realize that our love isn't typical. I don't think love should be typical. My family loves you. People want us to succeed. I want us to succeed." Thomas looked at Mary, then at the sky. He seemed troubled. Mary thought to herself.

"People?" Mary asked, surprised. She twirled a blade of grass.

"Those that know us. I mean that really know us. People that care about us. Your friend, Anna, Emily, Nellie, Huck, my folks. They want us to be happy together and we will. I'll be a doctor and you'll be a teacher, a good teacher at that. That will be our foundation and we will build from there. Mary Mascia, I love you like no other person in the world. My life would not be complete without you. Will you ... marry me?"

He took out a neatly wrapped ring. Mary took the ring and in awe, put it on her index finger. It was a perfect fit.

"Oh, Thomas! Of course! Thank you so much! It's absolutely beautiful!" Mary stood up and hugged Tom. The two of them slowly kissed. Love was stronger than the hate that tried to tear them apart. This handsome man, this educated, kindhearted, understanding man was going to be my husband, Mary thought to herself. She smiled like she never smiled in her life. Walking down the hill and holding hands. Endless opportunities filled Mary's mind as the newly engaged couple drove back to his home. This was a night to remember.

"Congratulations, kiddos!" Nellie exclaimed as she opened the door. Mary walked in holding Tom's hand gleefully. Marge and Frank both came in, giving the happy couple hugs.

"My new beautiful daughter-in-law to be! The ring looks more beautiful in person! You didn't describe it in full justice, Frank!" Marge excitedly said, her arms were covered in different bracelets which made a noise when she moved. "Oh, wait until the girls hear about this. The wedding could be next July. Oh dear, I'll have to lose a good 50 pounds by then."

Frank put his hand on his wife's shoulder. "Take it easy, Marge. Nellie drove to the bakery and picked up an Italian rum cake. I also have some champagne to celebrate!"

"I love Italian rum cake!" Mary said in excitement. The air was full of happiness and hope.

"I drove all the way to this bakery in Fort Wayne. It was made fresh. The young fellow said it makes all the young soldiers who return home from war happy, especially the rum part." Nellie smiled at the new couple. She knew it would work. " Now who wants a big old piece?"

The four of them stayed up till the morning. Mary and Thomas both talked about their goals, both short-term and long-term. The cake was rich with flavor and each bite got better and better. It was everyone but Mary's first time eating it. They all enjoyed the new treat. Frank suggested it be a part of the menu. They all laughed and savored the time spent together though Mary's happiness would be short lived.

TWENTY-FOUR

Today was the day Mary had been trying to avoid for the past two weeks. She would not see Thomas for a good four months Which to her seemed like an eternity. What would happen in those four months? Would her parents opposition be so strong that it would knock everything apart? Was their love strong enough to withstand that kind of persecution? As irrational as it was Mary questioned Tom's love for her. Would he give up the battle? Would he stay grounded? His love was for me. I was the one he was engaged to be married to. Not someone else. Would distance and time break apart a beautiful relationship? Mary's mind was in a chaotic mess of emotions. She tried to keep herself together as Thomas loaded her bags in the back of his car. The sky was gloomy, rain looked as if it was on its way.

The last of the bags was loaded. Frank and Marge were standing under the stoop of the doorway. Nellie had stepped outside and gave Mary a heartfelt hug. Marge and Frank followed her lead.

"It has been such a pleasure getting to know you. I wish you a safe return home, hopefully this old lady will still be kicking when you come back," Nellie said wiping a tear from her eyes. This reminded her of her brother's marriage to the colored girl. Although the marriage was beautiful in the end, the beginning was ugly as sin itself. I hope they succeed. Nellie thought to herself.

"You'll make a beautiful addition to the Donahue family. It's an honor to call you my future daughter-in-law," Marge spoke softly and wiped a tear from her eye.

"May God be with you on your ride home. I hope to see you again in the spring. You promise you'll ignore the nonsense and come on back."

"I promise." Mary grinned, feeling like she was on cloud nine.

"Thanks for coming down. I'm sure you are going to make a beautiful bride." Frank gave her a hug. He was going to miss this girl. There was just something about her that he would miss.

The tears swam down Mary's face. Nellie gave her a handkerchief to use.

"Please don't cry. You'll see all of us again soon. Don't you worry, Sugar," Nellie said in a good hearted tone.

"Our home is always welcome to you." Marge said, not wanting to see her go.

"You can move in tomorrow if you want. I'll charge you 75 dollars rent," Frank suggested trying to make a joke.

Marge slapped him gently. "Sweetheart, you wouldn't pay a dime."

Mary soaked up her surroundings, the kindness and the memories. "You have all been so kind. I don't deserve such kindness, really I don't."

Thomas stopped her. "Stop with the drama. You have a 7 p.m. train to catch. Let's go, Darling." He took her hand, but she refused, "Goodbye, everyone. You are permanent residents of my heart no matter what happens. I'll always remember the kindness you showed." Mary then sat in the front seat. In the rearview mirror, she could see them standing on the porch waving her goodbye.

Kind people did exist in this world. Back home in Connecticut; kind sincere people were a rarity, unlike unicorns, giants and mermaids which remained a part of Mary's childhood fantasies. Kind people were not some mythical wonder. They existed in a small off the beaten path town called Noblesville. Noblesville would become her new oasis. Mary and Tom talked about their new life together on the way to the train station. It was as if time slowed down and curtsied just for them.

The torrential rain was coming down hard. The drop-off was crowded with people. There was a long line and neither of them minded.

Mary nervously glanced out the foggy window . She was reticent about communicating her doubts to Thomas.

"Mary, this week was the happiest week, I've ever had in my life. I'm going to be your husband and you will be my wife.

That's amazing. I never thought that the beautiful woman I saw that night wearing the bright yellow dress would be mine forever." He gently embraced her.

"Tom, your family was so wonderful. I fell in love with the town from day one. Everything was just so wonderful." Mary's lips started to quiver.

"Baby, what's wrong?" Thomas caressed her hair.

"What's wrong is I'm going back to reality in 72 hours. A brutal reality. A reality where what I think and feel are totally ignored."

"Don't worry. We're engaged. It's final. It's a done deal," Thomas said, trying to convince her that everything was going to be okay. "I want you to go on that train with the realization that you are a new person. You are not the same Mary that came a few weeks ago. You have goals, you have plans, and you have a wedding to look forward to in the upcoming year."

Mary nodded her head in agreement.

"Now, you get on the train and get some rest. Also, remember that 800 miles away, a young man with ambition, loves you very much. You got this my friend."

Mary leaned over and gave him a long satisfying kiss goodbye. Though he seemed convinced, she wasn't so sure. It bothered her. She wanted the conviction that he had. She couldn't. She just could not share his conviction that everything was going to be okay. It seemed foolish.

In those two minutes, time stood still. Later that night, while trying to sleep in the rickety old train her last memory of him was seeing him wave goodbye as he pulled off to go. That face. That reassuring personality. Would she ever see him again? Would she ever see those wonderful people who referred to her as family? Ever again? Time would tell.

TWENTY-FIVE

The train arrived at Union Station at 11:30 p.m. on a gloomy Sunday night. Trying to carry two large suitcases full of clothes and belongings, Mary accidentally let go of one of them. The suitcase fell in front of a fellow passenger.

"Will you watch what you're doing?" the heavyset man with the fedora snapped. He glared angrily at her.

"I'm sorry, sir. I just had such an exhausting trip," Mary tried to apologize.

"Yeah, whatever lady." The man brushed her off and went his way.

It occurred to Mary that she was back home in Connecticut. The people here are so miserable, Mary thought to herself as she waited on the bench outside. Anna was supposed to pick her up since neither of her parents drove. She looked around at the stone-cold faces in her midst. This place was far from Noblesville. It seemed like she was in a different world. How do people live like this? Such a hostile bunch of people.

Suddenly, the sound of a truck interrupted her thoughts. It was Anna. She was all smiles.

"How is my Mary doing?" she asked, taking her suitcases from her. Mary gave her a hug, feeling loved, she sat in the front seat.

"So, let me see this ring!" Anna's brown eyes were aglow with happiness.

Mary showed her the ring. Both girls were ecstatic.

Mary looked at the depressing scenery of New Haven. The war really took a toll on her city. Everything looked so bleak and the buildings looked so run down. What had happened to the once glorious city she so much admired?

"Oh my, isn't that beautiful! I can't wait to hear about your trip," Anna remarked as she pulled in the front of Mary's house. It wasn't the nicest of homes, nonetheless it was hers. She had many nice memories at this house.

Mary was full of joy. "Thank you."

"I'll talk to you tomorrow." Anna waved goodbye.

The front door was peeling flakes of white paint. Her father was getting older, Mary thought to herself as she made her way up to the second-floor apartment. Each stair creaked. Something told her to take her time. A feeling of uneasiness was in the air.

She opened the door to reveal her mother just staring angrily at her. Her face had the look of pure wrath. Her father was seated in the background with his head in his hands, crying.

"Marie! No good! No good! Why you do this? You caused us so much pain!" Samuel said, crying hysterically.

Mary was in total shock. "What is going on?"

"GET OUT OF MY HOUSE!" Philomena screamed while picking up her suitcases and throwing them down the stairs, causing a loud disruption.

The first-floor door swung open. "What is going on? It's midnight. I'm trying to get some sleep!" Her neighbor then slammed the door, causing his 9-month-old girl to start screaming. "Just great!" He yelled through the thin walls.

"Mom! Dad!" Mary couldn't not process what was going on. Gina came out of her bedroom. She had a sly grin on her ruddy complexion.

"You ought to be ashamed of yourself! You have no clue the pain you caused our parents. They were worried sick about you! Who do you think you are? You can't cook! You don't clean! What kind of wife would you make? You know we're struggling, and you go all the way to Indiana when you know the pain you caused our parents!" Gina yelled.

"Marie! Marie! Why?" Her mother pleaded. She grabbed her hand sobbing. Cursing in Italian, she kept shaking her head.

"Why can't you be happy for me? It's all about you, isn't it?" Mary retorted. Samuel was shaking his head and cursing in Italian.

Gina stood right in front of her face. "Dad told you he didn't like Tom. You just went your own way!"

Gina smiled at Mary sheepishly. "Don't worry, Dad. I'll marry a rich handsome Italian man. I always obey my parents."

Samuel gave Mary a look of pain. He was deeply hurt.

"Gina, I love Tom and he loves me," Mary replied in a frustrated tone. "I'm sorry you don't understand how love works. None of you do."

"GET OUT!" Philomena scowled. She shoved Mary to the door and slammed it with all her might. Mary nearly fell down the stairs.

With no money and nowhere to go, the only place she could think of was Anna's. Thomas's words echoed in her mind: "A young man 800 miles away loves you." She also remembered Nellie's kind words: "You and Tom have forever together."

Making her way up to the stairs of Anna's house, Mary felt alone and lost. A cold gust of wind blew over her. Her family was in Noblesville. She had already missed the presence of Marge and Frank. She missed the grandmotherly affection of Nellie.

She gave the door a loud knock.

"Who is it?" Anna's voice could be heard through the door. "Who in heavens is it at such an hour?"

"It's Mary, can I come in?"

Anna opened the door. She was wearing a night gown and her long hair was in a braid.

"Come in, I figured it wouldn't go well. Let me make you some warm milk. You can sleep in the guest room. It's very late. and I have to be in school by 6:30 a.m."

"Sorry, I just had nowhere to go."

Mary felt like she was intruding. Anna read her vibes and gently put her hand on her shoulder.

"Don't apologize. We will talk in the morning."

Mary cried herself to sleep that stormy night. Her family's animosity towards Tom, the long distance between them, along with the uncertainties of whether such a marriage could survive all disproved the age-old belief that love concurs hate. The power of love would not win this battle. Like a dying fire that one is trying to keep going, Mary and Tom would try to rekindle their love for one another. Although in the end it simply was not meant to be.

It would be one long week before Philomena would allow her daughter to come back home. No mention of Tom was allowed in her house. However, a letter from Thomas Donahue would be a common sight whenever Samuel got the mail. Letters of love from the mysterious man from Noblesville, Indiana.

TWENTY-SIX

MODERN DAY

"And here you guys are today, 70 years later. This has been a truly remarkable night," Milagros exclaimed while helping Thomas get his coat on. The cable box read 10:00 p.m. Chester, the cat was sound asleep on Mary's lap. She had shed a few tears thinking about her past relationship with the man whom she most loved some seven decades prior.

"Here we are today," Mary smiled. "I still have that ring, too. I was the talk of the city. It was a most beautiful night. I'm so happy we were able to talk about the good old days. And Tom," she said looking at his weary face.

"Yes, Mary?" His voice shook with trembling. His blue eyes were red and puffy.

"You and I will remain good friends till the day we die. You have my number. Feel free to call anytime you like."

His whole demeanor lit up.

"I wish I could spend more time with you in person. I'm just so tired and weak. We may never meet again."

Milagros was standing by the door, wiping away tears from her eyes. She never would have imagined how beautiful this night would turn out to be. She stood there taking it all in.

Mary glanced at Milagros, then back at Tom.

"I know. That's why this meeting was made in heaven. I'm convinced that God gave you the strength to go to the bank. I often wondered what happened to you. Now I know. You lived a long rich life," Mary said with tears down her face.

Thomas smiled, "Now you know."

Mary nodded and softly said, "Now I know."

She gave him one last warm embrace. He was so frail. She knew this would be the last time they saw each other in person.

Milagros gave her a long, comforting hug. "Thank you so much for having us over. This night was a special night for all of us."

"My pleasure. You are more than welcome in my home anytime you please." She looked at Chester who lay sound asleep on her love seat. "It's just Chester and me."

"Keep the tiramisu coming, and I'll be here," Milagros joked. She was holding Thomas upright. He was clutching his walker.

"Will do, young lady." Mary smiled.

Milagros was touched by this encounter. To see two past lovers, reunite and act like nothing had happened was truly priceless. Tonight, was a night to remember. The two of them left that house feeling rejuvenated.

Mary closed the door behind. As was her custom, she wrote in her diary of her experience that night. In neatly written cursive, it read:

> *I knew one day I would grow old. I just never expected it to happen this fast. My 40s grew into my 50s, my 60s were full of good health, while my 70s saw some major health difficulties, my 80s showed me pains I never knew existed. I am now 90 years old. While most 90-year-olds are stored away in nursing homes, I am fortunate to live in the same Cape Cod that Albert and I bought back in 1955. There is nothing special about the house except that it was ours. My house is small and dainty, much like myself. If 90 years of life have taught me anything, it's to always keep busy and never stop learning. When I was 77, I learned how to paint. In my kitchen above the doorway is a little painting of a young woman engrossed in a book. In my 80s I learned how to cook. Sounds funny for an old Italian lady like myself to learn how to cook at 85, but never too late to learn. Now at 90, I have treasured my life for what it is and not for what it might have been.*
>
> *Signed,*
> *Mary Conti*

At that, Mary closed her diary, placed it in the nightstand by her bed with the pen neatly placed on top. She turned off her light and retired for the night.

TWENTY-SEVEN

OCTOBER 11, 2014

It's funny how much life changes in four years, Milagros thought to herself as she drove to Mary's house at 111 Overton rd. She had lost 40 pounds, graduated from nursing school, and had recently been engaged to a young man from Levittown. All good news she had wanted to share with Mary. Neither of them spoke to each other after that night. Milagros had wanted to befriend her; life had gotten in the way of things.

While most patients are just that, Thomas Donahue was more like an old beloved friend to Milagros. He had deteriorated badly in the past few months. He could no longer walk; his muscles had atrophied. He lay in his wheelchair with nothing but his mind working. It was a sad sight to see. She had wanted to let Mary know so she could visit him at Village West, a retirement home where Thomas had 24-hour care.

As she pulled up to the house, she noticed what appeared to be construction going on. There was a large dumpster in the driveway along with a contractor's work van that read Tile by Conti. A white Nissan Altima was parked behind it.

Curious, Milagros made her way to the front door, which had been replaced. She knocked on the door twice.

A middle-aged man with brown hair and dirty work clothes answered.

"How can I help you?" The man asked, seemingly in a hurry. He spoke in a gruff manner.

"My name is Milagros. I wanted to talk to Mary. Is she home?" Milagros asked, wondering what was up.

The man opened the screen door and shook her hand.

"My name is Paul. I'm sorry my mom passed away on March 24th. We are trying to fix up her place and put it back on the market. I would invite you in but it's a disaster inside."

The man looked down and tried to compose himself.

Milagros was stunned. She had appeared to be in such good health. Of course, that was four years ago.

"Oh my. I'm so sorry. She was such a sweet person. What happened? She seemed in such great shape for her age." Tears came down her face.

"My mother was an amazing person. She suffered a massive stroke back in January shortly after her 94th birthday. If you knew my mother, you knew she wasn't the type to live her life as an invalid, so she spiraled downhill rather quickly. She was 94, lived a long life. How did you know her? We're you a former student?"

"No. My patient was good friends with her many years ago. They met up at a bank. He's 98 and not doing too well. I wanted to come by and let her know. Also, I wanted to catch up. I knew I shouldn't have waited this long. Its just life has been hectic." Milagros shook her head in regret.

"My family thought we had many more years left with her too. It was a sudden loss. I'm just happy she was able to make it to my oldest son's wedding in December of last year. It's too bad. That would have been nice. I'm sure she would have loved to see you. It sounds like you guys bonded."

"You know, it was just for one evening. We never spoke after that. There was something about that evening which was so …" She paused, "memorable."

Paul nodded. "My mother had that gift. Once you met her, you never forgot her. She was quiet, so it took time to get to know her. Once people gave her a chance, they had a real friend and a mentor.

"Who is it? Tell them we're not interested." A loud, obnoxious voice appeared out of nowhere. An older Italian lady with short cropped reddish-brown hair appeared. She wore large glasses.

"Gina, this is Milagros. She knew Mary." Paul introduced her to Milagros.

"Pleased to meet you." Gina shook her hand, she was the total opposite of Mary.

"How did you know my sister?"

"Milagros was an aide to a friend of your sister," Paul explained, a little fidgety.

Gina raised her eyebrow. "Oh yeah. Who was it? A lot of her friends are long gone."

"Dr. Thomas Donahue," Milagros said quietly. She was curious to see what kind of reaction she would get.

There was a moment of stunned silence. She stood there, her mind racing with thoughts.

"Thomas who?" Paul asked with a puzzled expression.

"Donahue, he was your Mother's f…"

Milagros cut her off. "Friend. They knew each other back in college."

Paul shrugged his shoulders. "I don't know him. Listen, I would love to stay and chat. My wife and I were hoping to have the house ready by the 1st. I gotta run. Nice meeting you."

Milagros smiled. "Thank you sorry again for your loss."

"Thank you." Paul said softly before going back in the house. He closed the door and lowered the radio.

Gina turned to Milagros. She thought he was long gone by now.

"Is he still alive? He must be 105 if he is."

"He's 98 and not doing too good. That's why I wanted to come. I had hoped to take Mary to see him."

"Gosh, I thought he died years ago. Thomas Donahue was a phantom lover. No one knew what happened to him. She never spoke of him when she was married to Al. Back then there was no internet. There was no way of finding out what became of him. I would like to see him. Which facility is he in?"

"Village West. On Towers Road." Milagros replied.

"I'll stop by this afternoon. It's been years since I last saw him. For a while, he was all Mary spoke about. They would have made a cute couple. What can you do?" Gina shrugged her shoulders. "That's life."

"Did you ... Did you know about the letters?" Milagros asked, not sure if she did.

After a long pause, Gina replied. "Yes. I assume that's why Tom wanted to see her. I was the only person to know of that whole situation. She had wanted me to keep it a secret from Paul and Albert. She did not want to cause any drama in the family. It's a secret I was planning on taking to the grave. Even though she's gone, I just couldn't tell him. Everyone that knew about it is long gone. Her friend Anna passed in 2003. Her husband died of a massive heart attack back in '58. She lived to the envious age of 96. She had tried to coax Mary into telling Paul. She and Mary spoke a lot on the phone. I really do believe that she was Mary's only true friend. Mary just couldn't do it. It caused her too much pain. I think she always wondered what would have happened had they been married. She had a happy marriage. The thought always took residence in her mind."

"They were so beautifully written. You can tell the emotion in his words. I would have loved to see her responses. It's a shame. Life goes on." Milagros reminisced.

Gina shrugged her shoulders. "We wouldn't be standing here if they went through with it. I wouldn't have a wonderful nephew to help his 85-year-old aunt. Mary and Albert wouldn't have had almost 39 years together. "

Gina continued. "In all honesty, life would have been totally different had they kept the engagement. I owe him an apology for how my family treated him." As if she was the diplomat for her family.

"I don't think it would do him any good." Milagros said being realistic. "The damage is done."

Gina disagreed. "I think it would. When you're that old, I think it would give him peace of mind to know that what he went through wasn't right. I know it influenced my sister. She was never quite the same. I'm sure it affected him. Is he a widower?"

"No. He never married. He claimed that Mary was his one true love.

"That doesn't make any sense. He was a doctor, he had money, prestige. He could have had any girl he wanted," Gina noted.

"He wanted Mary. That was the girl who he loved. She was his world. And your parents gave her so much grief. Gave them so much grief, I should say."

Gina leaned on the banister. "Well, that was the past. I'm not proud of how my family treated him. I wasn't so kind myself. I was just following their suit. I was a dumb young girl who hated to see her mother and father cry their eyes out every night. My dad would drink his red wine in disgust. It really took a toll on them." She had almost seemed like she was trying to make what they did okay. There wasn't the slightest hint of remorse in her voice.

"You realize it was wrong? You're not trying to justify your actions. Your sister said you caused her a lot of pain. Racism is wrong, Gina. You and your family ruined what could have been a wonderful, happy, long-lasting marriage. You must admit that you, all three of you were wrong. I'm just not convinced that you feel you are. You weren't there that night. You didn't see the pain that I saw in both of their eyes. You weren't with Tom that night on the way home, when he was crying his eyes out. The pain you caused was unnecessary. You think that an apology is gonna fix this poor man's broken heart."

Milagros looked at her straight in the eye.

"Am I on trial? That was 60 plus years ago! Now I do. Now, as an old woman, I damn well know the pain my family caused. Back then I was blinded by my mother's old-world views. I know what I did was wrong. I should have defended her. I should have said, you know mom, she found someone better than you did. I didn't. I was too afraid to. There's no use in the what ifs. What time are visiting hours over at the nursing home?"

"11-8 p.m. If you want, I'll take you. He has Parkinson's and it's advanced to the point where all his muscles are weakened. His mind is still sharp. Just the other day, his niece was contemplating putting him in hospice care."

"The doctor said he has days, possibly weeks, but not months," Milagros added, wiping a tear from her brown eyes. She was going to miss him.

Gina shrugged her shoulders. "Do you really think he would remember me after all these years?" she asked, a tad hesitant.

"Tom is one exceptional man. I'm sure he would," Milagros replied.

"Well let's go. I would like to spend some alone time with him if you don't mind," Gina said in a stern tone.

"Sure." Milagros knew that this might just be what he needed. Almost as if the uncertainty of what happened had kept him alive all these years. Perhaps in some way Gina's admission of guilt, sincere or not, would finally give him the very permission to close his eyes in eternal rest.

Village West was a 450-room nursing home on the edge of town. It lay atop the hill. The building consisted of four floors. The fourth floor was hospice. The third was geriatrics. While the first two were for temporary rehab patients, the first two were up to date and modern. It gave the illusion of a beautiful facility. The third and fourth were as old and outdated as some of the people that resided there.

Milagros dropped Gina off the front of the building. Two elderly ladies in wheelchairs greeted her. Gina smiled and walked to the front desk. A morbidly obese lady with a name tag reading Beverly acknowledged her.

"Who do you wish to see?" the lady asked in a no-nonsense voice.

"Thomas Donahue," she replied. A young man pushing himself in a wheelchair asked to get by her. She moved over

"Room 311, Side B. You're going to take the elevator to the third floor. It will be down the hall way and to the far right. If you get lost, just ask one of the girls to help you. It's easy."

"Thank you." Gina walked down the hallway and took the elevator.

A young mother and her mourning 8-year-old son entered the elevator as she exited.

"Grandma is looking down at you now. Stop crying," she said as the door closed.

The strong stench of urine and vomit greeted Gina. Elderly people sat like drooping flowers in their wheelchairs. At one time much like Tom these people were young and spry full of ambition.

"Mr. Benson needs his insulin in 326, Side A." An older Haitian aide with the name tag that read Pauline, said "Stop texting your boyfriend and get him some insulin." She barked at one of the younger girls. The young girl rolled her eyes and went to Room 326.

"Miss, can you direct me to Tom Donahue's room?" Gina asked the aid.

"Follow me." The aide led her to his room. Gina and the aide walked past his roommate, a Jewish man in his 80s bedridden and on oxygen. The name tag on the door read Abraham Markowitz Side A. Thomas Donahue Side B.

"Mr. Donahue, you have company. This young lady wants to see you. Sit up in your chair." The aide announced.

He was seated in a quadriplegic wheelchair. A blue bib was underneath his gaunt chin. He was skin and bones. The frail ancient man turned his head to the aide. He looked totally unrecognizable to Gina. This is the curse of life she thought to herself. What a shame.

"Who is it? I don't see any young lady." He asked, coughing up a storm. He still had a sense of humor.

Gina bent down and shook his withered hand. "My name is Gina. I'm Mary Conti's sister." She then sat on the chair next to the TV. A news show was on. The volume was on full blast.

What little life he had lit up his face. "Mary? How is she? The last I saw her was a few years ago. I remember you. You got old." Tom smiled.

Gina laughed. "I'm 85. I feel pretty good though."

"You're a kid. I'm 98. I'll turn 99 next February. I doubt I'll make it. Will you please shut the TV off? Nothing but broken promises on CNN."

Gina turned the TV off.

"You remember me?" Gina asked genuinely surprised.

"Yes." Thomas replied.

"Gosh, it's been so long ago." Gina reminisced.

"I still have my mind. My body is gone. Old age is terrible. I can't do anything for myself anymore. My mind says go, my body says who are you kidding?"

"Tell me about it." Gina chuckled. She sat on the edge of his bed. Empty bowls of food and a carton container of apple juice was on his tray next to the bed.

"Is Mary here?" Thomas asked hopefully. He piped up.

"No. She's resting now." Gina said, hoping he didn't put two and two together.

"I could use some rest myself. I will after you leave. Please stay a while. It's great to see you."

"I won't stay too long." Gina noticed an old color photo of her sister wearing a beautiful yellow satin dress, her face was illuminated in pure happiness. Tom held her arm as they looked toward the future.

"My sister looked so beautiful in that dress, look at how handsome you were too. At 98, you still look good." Gina picked up the photo and smiled down at it.

"It beats the alternative. I remember that night like it was yesterday." He coughed his throat. "How did Al treat your sister? I always wondered. Was he good to her? I don't think it's possible for any man to love her more than I did. I really thought that she was the one."

"Tom, you were her first true love. Mary really loved you. What we did to you was wrong. Al was a great guy. It was a rough start at first. In the end, they were happy. They were married for almost forty years. I always felt like he was God's Plan B. You were the one she really related to. You took such good care of her. She spoke highly of how you and your family treated her. You guys treated her right. We were the ones who were in the wrong. We weren't loving to her. Or to you for that matter. Do you accept my apology? I realize it's unfixable the pain we caused you."

Thomas struggled to get his voice out. "How can I hold you accountable for how your folks felt about me? That wouldn't be right. All three of us were young and dumb. I should have known that a long-distance relationship would not work. You should have stood up for her. Mary should have done what she wanted. We tried so hard. We tried so … hard! And our efforts just fell apart."

"It wasn't in vain. Love is never in vain. You guys tried your best and that's what mattered." Gina responded.

"We didn't. We were both foolish. I should have never left Yale. I should have stayed in Connecticut and got my degree there. I was so sure that a long-distance relationship could work. I thought love was stronger than hatred. It isn't. That kind of regret is a lot to carry all these years, you know?"

"No use worrying about it now."

"I know. You know, I had money, a job I loved. And for most of my life, I had great health. One thing I never had was happiness. Only the right kind of woman can make a man truly complete. I never had that. I always wondered if she felt the same."

"Don't worry about stuff like that," Gina said trying to be of comfort.

"I know you mean well. I'm afraid you'll never understand. Everyone deserves to be married. No one should live for almost a century as a loner. Not when the woman of his dreams was engaged to be married to him."

Gina pat him gently on the shoulder. "It's okay. It's in the past."

Suddenly. His voice got stronger. His now dull eyes appeared full of emotion.

"It is a human right to be married. I never had a son to teach how to ride a bike. Or had the privilege of watching my child's first steps. I never had the honor of attending my son or daughter's wedding. Morons nowadays have children. They have privileges that I never had. I call them morons because I see them all the time on these television self-help shows. They have no clue how to raise their kids. I was denied my right to be a potential father thanks to your family. And now that I'm old and decrepit and near death, I don't even have grandchildren to come visit me in my dying state. I was looking forward to have grandkids to teach and educate. I was looking forward to seeing their little minds develop into young brilliant people. Thanks to the relentless rubbish your family put me through, I have none of that. My roommate has grandkids that come visit him every single day after work. I get no one. My niece visits me on the holidays. They roll me downstairs and spend a half hour with me, if that. Your family did a number on me. And you say everything is okay? It sure isn't."

Gina just sat there, not sure of what to say.

The old man continued his thought. "But, as my friend used to preach in his sermons, forgive and forget. I must forgive the ignorance of your family. I must forgive their fears about me and Mary. Whether they were irrational or not. Lastly, I must forget and move on. That's something I have tried to do for the last 65 years. Forget about Mary. Forget about the hatred, the late nights we spent together talking in my parent's house. I must forget all the good times we reminisced about years ago on that glorious night. I must forget and move on. At 98, I can finally say I'm ready."

"No. Don't forget the good times. Forget the stupidity. Forget my parent's lack of understanding. They never understood the kind of man you are."

Gina gave him a hug. "Never forget the good times of life. That's what made you who you are. You've had 98 years of great memories. Don't let two to three years ruin it."

Thomas got all choked up. "Thank you. I needed to hear that."

Gina smiled. "You're welcome."

"I have to get going. I have to make supper. I'm making Chicken Genovese. Wanna come over? Dinner is at 7?" she joked.

"Sure. It sounds better than the slop they give us here. Unfortunately, I'm stuck here. Thanks for the invite."

"You're very welcome. Listen, take care of yourself and I'll see you soon." Gina patted his withered hand. Deep down, she knew it would be their last meet up.

"See you soon," he whispered. He managed to smile.

Gina walked past the other patient, when Thomas struggled to call her name.

"Gina!"

She turned around.

"Thank you. Today was a great sense of healing for me. I've waited many years for this Day of Reconciliation. I'm finally ready to move on."

"Don't you go anywhere now. We got to plan something for your 100th," Gina laughed.

Thomas smiled. "No, I'm not going anywhere. I'm finally ready to forgive and move on with my life. I'll expect some of your gourmet cooking and a bottle of bourbon for my 100th."

Gina chuckled. "You bet. Take care, dear."

"See you soon. Give my regards to Mary."

Gina paused and replied, "You'll be seeing her soon. See you again my friend."

"Goodbye. Take care dear." Thomas said in a relaxed tone.

It gave him comfort in knowing that the love of his life was well cared for. For almost 70 years, Thomas wondered what happened to the beautiful woman in the bright yellow dress after they went their ways. Would she be happy?

Did the man she married love and respect her as she should be treated?

He could now be at peace. Exhausted from the medication, Thomas lay his head back in his chair and drifted off to a deep sleep. His agile mind was filled with memories of him and Mary. He found peace. He could now rest.

Three hours later

"Mr. Donahue. Time to take your Benztropine." Odessa, the nurse, twice glanced at the motionless man slumped over his wheelchair. He was dead. In his hands was the photo of him and Mary. She took the photo and placed it on the table next to his bedside. She rang for help. To her, it was just a typical old man looking at his past youth. To her, it was another ancient relic of the good old days who passed on. She had not known of the story of Mary and Tom. A love story that could not be. A relationship lost to the sands of time.

The marriage of Mary and Tom, a story that was conceived but never came to birth.

Author's Note

I was ten years old when my mother found the collection of 134 love letters from Thomas Donahue to Mary Mascia. Mary was my grandmother whom I never knew. She passed away just two weeks shy of my birth on November 2, 1988.

I was 16 years old when I first heard of the story of what happened. Her sister told me of Mary's struggle to please her parents while being in love with the soon to be Dr. Donahue. She spoke of the town's support for the two of them. While some of the names were changed, the characters in this book were based from real people. Her best friend was a Jewish teacher whom lived near her home. Her father really did have his own paradise-like garden in the back of his home. She really did write to Eleanor Roosevelt and Mahatma Gandhi.

We don't know for sure what transpired between the two of them. We don't know why she kept these letters hidden all these years. Or if she even communicated with him in the past shortly after it took place. I have always wanted to write my own novel. When I heard of this true-life love story, I just had to share it with the rest of the world.

I encourage all my readers to do their own research and look up their own genealogy. I guarantee that somewhere along the lines there is a story that could easily be told.

Acknowledgements

During the nearly two and half years to write this book, two people have been of extraordinary help. I would like to thank my father, Joseph Fonte, for his help in making sure I captured the personality of his family thru the written word.

I would also like to give my sincere appreciation to my co-worker, Ciro Festa, who helped me in the translation of my great grandparent's conversation in authentic Italian. Both gentlemen, along with many others in my life, have been of utmost support in accomplishing my life long dream of becoming an American novelist.

The Letters

Below are a sample of the letters that were written between an emotionally anguished Tom and his fiancé, Mary.

May 30, 1944 - Plans for life as a couple.
June 5, 1944 - Invitation to Indiana.
June 9, 1944 - Referring to the party.
July 20, 1944 - Thomas' response to Mary's letter to his father.
August 24, 1944 - Difficulties in relationship.
September 4, 1944 - Tom's reaction to Mary's letter.
September 8, 1944 - Depression, lack of parents understanding.
September 27, 1944 - Thomas coming to acceptance.

Plans for life as a couple.

Tues., May 30 —

My dearest —

You've made me very very happy, my darling, by saying what you said in this last letter. That's what I've been hoping more than anything to hear from you, and now that both of us know what we want, it would be nice to start making some plans. You see, sweet, when I love a person as I love you, it's very hard to have to be away so far and for so long, when I know how happy I would be if you were here with me. I've been quite sure that I made that all-important decision, and now I realize more than ever that life without you could never be complete. There had always been a girl in my dreams, Mary — you know — someone interested in the same things as I, intelligent, beautiful as well as very attractive, and aware of some of the problems that need to be solved. I really never expected to find all these qualities combined in one girl, and when I knew I had, I decided my search was all over, and now I'm more sure than ever.

So now shall we make some plans about seeing each other this summer, and then we can talk things over and set the date? There are lots of problems to think of, and it will be so wonderful to be with you again and be able to tell you in person how much I love you. It's been 5 months, sweetheart, and they've seemed more like years. Some day we'll have a beautiful home, a lovely family, and we'll travel, too, Mary, and do so many of the things we always liked to talk about. Maybe we could even teach each other some Russian, and could spend some time studying and travelling over there. I know it's something I'd like to do. Still, back to the immediate future — If our furlough is long enough, I'll plan to come back there, but if not, I'll send money and I want you to come out here. What do you think? Answer soon, hon — Love always
Tom

Invitation to Indiana

Mon., June 5 —

My dearest —

I only wish there was something definite about this furlough business. All we know is that we will get one, and that it will start June 27th or so, but nobody seems to know for how long. General opinion is that it will be for only 6 or 7 days. So I don't know what to count on. Sweetheart — could your mother object too much if she knew you were coming to see your fiancée — or does she know yet? The length of time we get off isn't up to our officers alone, but is determined by the date that classes start for the 2d semester — it's supposed to be around the 1st of July, so you see that wouldn't allow much time to see you, figuring 3 days travel time for the round trip. I've missed you so very much, darling, and I want to make the most of every minute I do have off. Maybe we'll have all the angles considered by the time tests are over — what would make me very happy would be for you to step off the train the very moment my last final is over — maybe this is just wishful thinking — whatever happens, I want above everything to be with you then and always.

Mary, every once in a while I read something in one of your letters that just suggests there's something you want to say, but hesitate to for some reason or other. Perhaps I'm wrong, but I get that feeling. Maybe you'd rather wait and talk about it. I think we can be very much more personal and intimate in our next conversations.

Will your folks object to your getting married, hon — My own always said they'd rather I'd wait until my education is over, but personal happiness means so much, and it seems so long already since we've been together. Life would hold so much more for me if you were here beside me. I really need you, darling, and want you more than anything else in all the world. You see, you turned out to be the girl I'd always dreamed about, and I don't want those dreams to fade away. You know you might come out to stay, and next furlough in November, we could both visit back east. What do you think? Answer soon, sweet.

always yours
Tom —

Referring to the party.

Fri., June 9 —

My dearest —

I think I owe a lot to the girl from Alaska, too. For it's because of her that I met the most wonderful girl I've ever known or hope to know. Isn't it funny how two people meet. Mary, at the party, I noticed you right at first, but thought you had a date with the fellow you were with, so that was that. For some reason or other, I couldn't get very interested in the evening's activities, and by the time the thing was breaking up, I was sorta' let down — but then I met you, and everything was just swell from then on. It was a real pleasure being with you, and I looked forward to every week-end with anticipation. How happy I'd been if I could have stayed at Yale and been there close to you all this time! Sweetheart, I've missed you so.

Mary, what I had in mind yesterday when I said we might kill two birds with one stone was this. You might come out here to

work this summer, we could be married, and could send money to your folks, too. I have around $200 saved, and could borrow from my brother if needed. At least it's an idea, and would make me very happy. The longest furlough I can possibly get can be only 6 or 7 days, and counting 3 days off for travel, it just dwindles away to nothing. But 3 days with you would be 72 hrs. of Heaven. If you should come out here, darling, then we'd have time enough to find a place to live, and could have a whole week of just us together, with no classes or anything interrupting. Hon, I don't want to be selfish, so if there are reasons why this wouldn't be satisfactory, please don't hesitate. I'm a pretty understanding soul, and there may be many other things I couldn't think of. But I know how very happy we could be together, and how hard it is to be so many miles from you for so long.
Write soon, sweet — all my love
Tom

Thurs., July 13 —

My dearest —

If this suddenly becomes illegible, please excuse it — I've been writing for about 2½ hrs. getting material from Gray's anatomy on the nerves, muscles and vessels of the thigh. We have an oral demonstration tomorrow to explain our dissection, and a good preparation is essential to make a good impression.

Sweetheart, I'm glad to know that you don't feel your folks will object to our marriage on religious grounds. In many cases, that's quite a serious issue, and I didn't want it to stand in our way. But I do hope their attitude about our date will change, because I want so much to have you with me, and it won't be at all necessary to wait any longer. We both know what we want. Strained relations with parents and in-laws are never good, however, so I hope they'll try to understand the situation. I guess the new generation finds it very difficult to reason with the old, and in our own case, the differences government. The shift shows that the Japs are becoming restless and doubtful of the out come.

And of course the big interest on the home front is the Democratic convention. We've been listening to it all our spare moments - it must be quite a thing. I'm only hoping that Wallace will have powerful enough support to win the nomination for vice-president again. His supporters wanted to nominate tonight, but Jackson adjourned over their protests. Tomorrow should be another big day. Quentin Reynolds & Roosevelt both spoke tonight, and I thought both made some very pertinent, as well as logical, points. I'm still of the belief that Dewey won't come close, but a lot depends on these next weeks before election time.

Darling, my dad mentioned your letter, and told me how very happy he was to hear from you. I'm so glad you wrote him - he appreciates things like that more than a little, and I know he'll enjoy corresponding with you.

What sort of plans do you have, as long as you don't think we'll be married this fall? I know a guy who's going to be very lonely all those months. I always think, though, that maybe by fall, your folks could change their attitude. I suppose that's Goodnight, my love wishful thinking. Tom

Thomas' response to Mary's letter to his father.

> Thurs., July 20—
>
> My dearest—
>
> This month of July is producing so many critical developments in both war and politics, at home and abroad, that it will be some time before the real significance is known. But it's certainly indicative of the coming course of events, I think. I just wonder how much longer those Russians will be able to keep driving on before they'll have to pull up and re-establish supply routes. I think they'll complete the fight for those 5 key cities they're now beginning before they cease, but I'm hoping they'll be able to keep going right on the road to Warsaw and Berlin.
>
> The latest attempt on Hitler's life will probably result in a rather bloody purge of Germany itself. Hitler's appointment of Heinrich Himmler and his Gestapo to handle the situation would make me expect that, at least.
>
> I don't know what to make of the change in the Japanese

government. The shift shows that the Japs are becoming restless and doubtful of the out come.

And of course the big interest on the home front is the Democratic convention. We've been listening to it all our spare moments — it must be quite a thing. I'm only hoping that Wallace will have powerful enough support to win the nomination for vice-president again. His supporters wanted to nominate tonight, but Jackson adjourned over their protests. Tomorrow should be another big day. Quentin Reynolds & Roosevelt both spoke tonight, and I thought both made some very pertinent, as well as logical, points. I'm still of the belief that Dewey won't come close, but a lot depends on these next weeks before election time.

Darling, my dad mentioned your letter, and told me how very happy he was to hear from you. I'm so glad you wrote him. He appreciates things like that more than a little, and I know he'll enjoy corresponding with you.

What sort of plans do you have, as long as you don't think we'll be married this fall? I know a guy who's going to be very lonely all those months. I always think, though, that maybe by fall, your folks could change their attitude. I suppose that's wishful thinking. Goodnight, my love.

Tom

230

Fri., July 21

my dearest —

I'm disappointed with the results of the Democratic vice-presidential nomination — another example of throwing away the liberal element to appease a reactionary group. I don't know a whole lot about Truman himself — except that he is a compromise candidate — that's grounds enough for my objection. I liked Wallace very much and hated to see him lose out. One great point that will be made against Truman is his one time association with the notorious Pendergast machine in Kansas City, Mo. Perhaps you've read about it several years ago. Well, I'd be willing to accept almost anyone before Dewey and Bricker. What a team the Old Guard put before the American voter! It shows that the extreme conservatism still reigns supreme in Republican ranks — such calibre men as McCormick still have too much influence on party doctrine and political maneuverings.

Some day when we travel in Russia, I'd seriously like to make an extensive study of the finer details of government organization and function there. Surely some of their ideas will be accepted by Americans in the future. I hope so, anyhow.

I hope your mother did like the gift. It's very hard to choose anything, but I wanted to be sure to get her something for being so generous and nice. My mouth still waters every time I think of her cookery. I just wish your folks didn't object to a free wedding. I'm not sure I understand their reasons, but I suppose it's useless to wonder. I always think of it, and secretly hope they'll change their mind.

This German internal problem may assume drastic proportions soon — it's at a critical time, so it could be a very important factor in the coming victory. Max Werner may turn out correct yet. Would a peace in Europe by fall affect our own plans any? At all, I hope it would hasten them. I want you so very much, my darling, and I need you, too. This way, I can't do my best — there's something lacking that I can't supply the way it is. Love always, my dearest

Ann

DIFFICULTIES IN RELATIONSHIP.

> Thurs., Aug. 24 —
>
> My dearest Mary —
>
> I've hesitated to write since I got your last two letters, but I think I've had plenty of time by now to test my reaction. Naturally, I'm disappointed at the impossibility of a fall wedding, but realizing all the time that the chances were slim made it much less difficult to accept. If both of us could be happy — reasonably so — away from each other, then it is probably wise to wait, but for a long time this summer I was really miserable. You can understand how important it is that we see each other again soon. What kind of urging and coercion are you trying, and for what compromise? I hope you're successful if it will help bring us together again. Darling, we've had lots of problems to think about but some day maybe we'll enjoy happy times together much more as a result of having had to face problems and solve them.
>
> I hope you'll forgive the brevity. I promise a much better letter soon. When do you start teaching? Write me all about it. I love you very much
>
> Tom.

Tom's reaction to Mary's letter.

Mon., Sept. 4 —

My dearest —

Darling, sometimes I have a very hard time trying to figure you out. First, I get a letter full of depression and doubt and a note of indecision, and then the next day one at the other end of the pole explaining the other letter — it's really quite confusing. But it's so hard trying to understand what's going on in a person's mind from reading written words — they never convey the deeper meanings. It's just that at times there seems to be a little doubt in your mind as to the wisdom of our getting married, and to me that reflects the idea that you may not want it yourself as much as I'd like you to. Do I misinterpret? Darling, I hope I do, but marriage is an undertaking which demands more assurance - on both sides - than almost anything else. That's why some of the things you write disturb me. Is there something you're trying to lead up to but can't quite say, or is my psychology gone astray? I'm as sure as I ever was about wanting you, but when I feel you're not so sure, it makes me wonder, and tends to create doubts in my own mind. So sweetheart, if there's something bothering you, please tell me, and working it out will make it much easier for both of us. I hope I haven't got off on a side-track somewhere in all this, but things you've written at different times have made me do some thinking.

Dearest Mary, don't ever doubt my feeling toward you - if we're to be married, I just want to be sure that feeling is reciprocated. Is that selfish? I miss you so very much, my love
always yours - Tom -

Depression, lack of parent's understanding.

Fri., Sept. 8—

My dearest Mary—

I've been in a black mood for several days past, and wouldn't write while I was feeling that way just because I didn't know what I wanted to say. Then last night I guess I reached the peak of this morbid state and decided to write anyway, but I left the letter unsealed and today I wouldn't mail it because I knew the things I said I didn't really mean at all. Maybe this is all very confusing to you, but I won't elaborate for fear of being misunderstood. What bothers me is the fear that by some means or other this extended engagement will result in our not being married at all, and I hate to even think of that, my dearest, because I'll always want you and miss you no matter what happens. If the distance factor weren't such an insurmountable obstacle so we could see each other often, the problem would be much less acute, but the way it is, seeing each other only once every four months or more doesn't seem to be working out so well. I just wish it were possible to make your folks understand so we could go ahead and be married this fall as we'd hoped. I'll never get over the disappointment of being told it couldn't be, and continually hope something will happen so we can do as we want to do. Is it all your folks, sweetheart, or are there other good reasons you've never written about? Sometimes I feel there must be, but I hope I'm wrong. I'm sure I was right, as far as I'm personally concerned, at least, about the feeling of insecurity and uncertainness this having to wait brings on. I can't get interested in anything, even my school work, and that's no good. Write soon, my darling, and please try to understand I've wanted to write every day but knew I'd better not. All my love, Tom —

Thomas coming to acceptance.

Mon., Sept. 27

Dear Mary —

I hope you'll forgive my negligence in getting this written — I've neglected my correspondence terribly the last week. My mother wondered if something had happened to me, so that made me realize I'd better get caught up with everyone. My German test is safely out of the way, and I'm thankful it was as easy as it was. My worries in that course are all over now.

for a German counter-offensive later on, but I hope it's never given a chance to develop.

How are all the little students coming along under your tutelage? I'm sure you have the situation well in hand.

We've finally had to put on our O.D.'s, the green ones, you know, so next time you see me, just shut your eyes for a few minutes and try to get over that first impression.

Two of my room-mates

Are you keeping up on the Russian news these past ten days. If I don't read the papers every day now, they have so many new cities captured that I don't know where they are. I thought surely the Nazis would make a great stand at Smolensk, and possibly mire the Russian drive down. Now it looks as if the Reds won't be stopped before the Polish border is reached. This Nazi retreat may be a German tactic to get the Russians to overextend their supply lines, so I'm looking drew details for this coming week-end, so they can't make the trip to New York. They're pretty disgusted and their morale is all shot. What do you suggest I do to help them out?

Well, it's time to run for class, so I'd hope for an answer soon.

Tom

CPSIA information can be obtained
at www.ICGtesting.com
Printed in the USA
LVHW010322270420
654483LV00005B/991